FUCK BUDDY

Scott Hildreth

This book is a work of fiction. Names, characters, places, and incidents are the product of the author's imagination or are used fictitiously. Any resemblances to actual events, locales, or persons living or dead, are coincidental.

Copyright © 2016 by Scott Hildreth

All rights reserved. In accordance with the U.S. Copyright Act of 1976, the scanning, uploading, and electronic sharing of any part of this book without the permission of the author or publisher constitute unlawful piracy and theft of the author's intellectual property. If you would like to use the material from the book (other than for review purposes), prior written permission must be obtained by contacting the author at designconceptswichita@gmail.com. Thank you for your support of the author's rights.

Published by
Eralde Publishing

Cover Design Copyright © Creative Book Concepts
Text Copyright © Scott Hildreth
Formatting by Creative Book Concepts

ISBN 13: 978-0692649305
All Rights Reserved

DEDICATION

To have a lover is one thing. To have a best friend is another. To have your best friend and your lover happen to be the same person is magical.

This book is dedicated to anyone who has had the luxury of falling in love with their best friend. There's nothing on this earth that can compare.

PROLOGUE

With my face buried in my pillow, I cried quietly, hoping not to wake either of my parents. I never would have guessed girls in fourth grade could be so hateful.

A light tapping on my window startled me. I wiped my tears on the shoulder of my nightgown, tugged the wrinkles from the fabric, and walked to the window. After pulling the curtains to the side and peering through the glass, his smiling face caused me to do the same.

"Open the window," he whispered.

I turned the lock, pushed against the frame carefully, and stepped to the side.

He grinned and pressed his finger to his lips. "Shhh."

"Okay," I whispered.

"Bad day, huh?" he said as he climbed in the window.

I chewed against my bottom lip, embarrassed for the tears I continued to shed. "Yeah."

"Girls are stupid." He brushed his long blonde hair away from his eyes. "Except for you."

"Boys are stupid, too."

"Are you still sad?" he asked.

I nodded.

As we both stood at the side of the bed, he held out his hand.

I took his hand in mine and squeezed tightly. Together, we fell onto the bed, hand-in-hand. He was different than the other boys. He was different than everybody. We were best friends, and one day I hoped he would ask me to be his girlfriend.

We silently laid on our backs holding hands for some time. I stared up at the glow-in-the-dark stars on my ceiling until I gathered the courage to speak. When I finally developed the nerve, I turned my head to the side. He did the same.

"Do you want to be my boyfriend?" I asked.

He shook his head. "Not yet."

I rolled my head to the side and gazed up at the ceiling, feeling foolish for having asked.

"But I'll be your best friend forever," he said.

"Pinky promise?" I asked.

He extended his pinkie.

I did the same.

And we swore.

Best friends for life.

CHAPTER ONE

OLIVIA

"Since when do you not have yogurt in here?" he asked.

I tossed the empty cottage cheese container into the trash and glanced over my shoulder. "Since you ate the last of it yesterday. I'll get some more when I go to the store."

Standing barefoot with his head shoved so deep into the refrigerator it was well out of view, Luke looked the way he did on any other day. Dressed in board shorts and an old tee shirt, at first glance he resembled most of the other surfers in southern California. His skin was deep bronze in color and he had the muscular structure of an athlete. With his handsome looks and a tasteful sleeve of tattoos down to one wrist, he could have had a career as a model if he chose to. Instead, he spent his time surfing and building the occasional custom surfboard for whoever he deemed worthy of his time and effort.

"I wasn't here yesterday." He cleared his throat and pushed the refrigerator door closed. "And if I would have taken the last one I would have said something."

As he turned around, his hair fell into his face. Long and brown with occasional strands of dirty blonde from exposure to the sun, it was one of his many appealing features, but arguably not his most attractive. He brushed it away from his eyes as he walked past me and toward the wire basket of fruit sitting on the kitchen counter.

I tried to remember when he ate the last cup of yogurt. "Those aren't oranges, they're Cara Cara's, the pink ones."

"Even better," he responded. "I love these things."

My coffee in one hand, and my bowl of cottage cheese in the other, I grinned. "Me too."

He tossed his head toward the countertop. "You're out of oranges, Liv."

With my mind still slightly foggy from my previous night's drunken escapade, I stood and stared at him, slightly jealous of his late winter tan. I envied the color of his skin, but realized when we were much younger that there was nothing I could do to ever become as dark as he was. With a mother who was half-Japanese and half-Chilean, and a southern California native for a father, he and his three siblings were adorned with an odd mixture of skin tones and hair colors. One of his sisters had light reddish-brown hair and the other a much lighter dirty-blonde, but both were fair skinned. His younger brother's hair was brown, and he had a very dark complexion similar to Luke's.

"See how I did that?" he asked.

"What? Grabbed the oranges?"

"No, told you I was eating the last one. I'm polite like that."

I cocked my head to the side and watched him pick at the peel of the orange with his thumb as he walked past me and toward the living room.

Grinning at my memory of the *Mission Beach Surf Shop* tee shirt he was wearing, I followed him into the living room. Several years prior, we had spent a day at the beach – he surfed and I baked in the sun – and when it was time to go, his shirt was nowhere to be found. The restaurant on the boardwalk wouldn't let him in without one, so we went to the adjacent surf shop to buy one. Initially we argued about the color of the shirt – he claimed it was a shade of gray, and I swore it was light pink. We both loved how the shirt fit him, so he bought it regardless. The comments that followed further confirmed his colorblindness, but everyone that knew him was fully aware of his deficiency when it came to identifying colors.

I sat down at the end of the couch. "So, how was surfing yesterday?"

San Diego's population was 1.5 million, but even as populated as it was Luke was well-known as a surfer. He was better than almost everyone in southern California and without a doubt could surf professionally, but he refused to do so. To him, surfing was sacred and would never be turned into a sport or competition. Somewhat of a local celebrity – and the recipient of more offers from women than he could possibly act upon – he chose to be single immediately following the breakup with his one and only girlfriend. He was twenty years old at the time.

As much as he was able, Luke lived a life of solitude and kept to himself. I had been in and out of many relationships, none worth the time I devoted to them, and not a single one produced a fraction of the satisfaction my friendship with Luke did.

Outsiders viewed him as antisocial, withdrawn and unfriendly, but they didn't know him the way I did. I understood why he was the way he was, and further knew him as being none of those things. Luke was kind, caring, funny, and wanted nothing more than to be allowed to live life in the manner he was comfortable with.

It didn't matter if a person knew Luke well or simply encountered him by chance, everyone agreed.

Luke was different.

He stopped in front of me and began to peel one of the oranges while resting the other between his upper arm and chest. He glanced up, met my gaze, and caught me admiring the few day's growth of beard on his face.

"First things first. The date, let's hear it," he said.

I did my best to change the subject. "I like the little beard thing you've got going on."

"I haven't had time to shave, it'll be gone tomorrow," he said dryly. "The date, Liv. Spill it."

Although I found cottage cheese grotesque to look at or think about, I always enjoyed eating it. I stared blankly into my bowl as I considered how much of the previous night's events I wished to share with him. The longer I studied the small curds, the less I wanted to eat it, and the more disgusted I became over my failed date. I set the bowl on the table and picked up my cup of coffee as he turned toward the kitchen. In a moment, he returned with both oranges peeled, separating one of them into sections as he glared at me.

I wrapped my hands around the warm porcelain cup and peered toward the bowl of spoiled milk curds. "Cottage cheese is so ugly."

He slipped a section of fruit into his mouth, and upon swallowing it, cleared his throat as if to demand my attention. "The. Date."

I raised the cup to my mouth and tilted my head back slightly as I took a drink. As I met his gaze, he pressed against the orange with both thumbs, pulled another section free, and poked it past his lips with the tip of his finger. As he chewed, he playfully tossed the uneaten orange into the air and caught in the other hand without shifting his eyes away from mine. Everything he did, he did with grace. I sometimes wondered if it was the martial arts his father made him study when we were kids or if it was the surfing that made his movements so fluid like. Whatever it was, I was grateful for it – watching him do almost anything was pleasurable.

Although I felt I needed to drink the entire cup of coffee, I lowered my cup and smiled. He cocked one eyebrow and pulled another section of orange free. I sighed heavily as if disgusted to talk about the date. To be brutally honest, I was.

"We met at the bar," I said. "He was married, and I left after maybe twenty minutes."

He widened his eyes as the side of his mouth curled up slightly. "That's it? You texted me a fucking thesis last night and you've sworn off Tinder because of *that*?"

I stared blankly at his bare feet. Even his toes were perfect. I glanced at my feet. Little sausage-like stubs surrounded the tips of my sandals. I had a reasonable amount of self-esteem, and I was well aware that I was pretty, but there was no doubt my fat little toes would prevent me from joining Luke if he ever chose a career in modeling.

"Well, it was just, I don't know. I think maybe I reached a point that all the lies and the bullshit were just too much. I'm sick of it. You know, every guy I met on there was a liar."

He poked the last piece of fruit into his mouth. "You're meeting people you don't even know. Men who can claim to be anyone or anything. All they want is to get laid. What did you really expect?"

How about great sex and a wedding ring?

He walked to the kitchen and quickly returned, flopping down on the couch beside me. I sat and sipped my coffee, not sure if I even wanted to answer his question. I had tried online dating on and off for the last four years, and in the past year had been on no less than a dozen dates from my *Tinder matches* alone. From a relationship standpoint my life was an absolute disaster.

For a long moment he glared at me, which was something he often did when he wanted me to continue talking about something I wasn't necessarily willing to talk about. Eventually he grew tired of waiting and broke the silence. "Really? That's it? Nothing weird or funny happened?"

Lacking the desire to continue talking about it, I sat silently, hoping it would satisfy him enough to move on to another subject.

"How'd you figure out he was married?" he asked.

I set my cup of coffee down and picked up the bowl. One glance at the cottage cheese and I felt like I was going to barf. The three hours of grieving after my botched date was wreaking havoc on my stomach. I had come home angry and disappointed with myself. A bottle of wine and two romantic comedies later and I was ready for bed – and to swear off dating. Lying in bed, half-drunk and irritated, I texted Luke a few rambling paragraphs explaining my disappointment with mankind in general.

I extended my arm and offered him the cottage cheese. "You want this?"

He shook his head lightly as he reached for the bowl. "I'll eat it. But what I want is for you to answer the question. All of a sudden you're *done dating*, and all you can say is that he was married."

I gave my signature response. I shrugged.

"He sure wasn't the first married guy you met on there."

"It's just…I don't…I don't know," I stammered. "He was so perfect. He had a great job, a nice car, seemed to have his shit together, and he was so fucking good looking."

"A hot married guy." He chuckled.

I nodded. "I just kept staring at him, thinking it was all too good to be true. I guess in the end, it was."

"Sorry it didn't work out."

I pursed my lips and shrugged in return.

"So, once again, how'd you find out he was married?"

I tapped my index finger against the ring finger of my left hand. "His ring finger had an indentation on it from his wedding ring. I noticed it, asked, and he answered truthfully. He said they were *arguing*. I mean, really. Who doesn't argue?"

"Everyone argues," he replied.

I shrugged. Again.

"Other than being married he sounds perfect," he said in a sarcastic tone.

Yeah, he was. He reminded me a lot of you.

CHAPTER TWO

LUKE

My incompatibility with others made coexistence almost impossible, however, living a life free of conflict was simple for me. I had one true friend, I rarely offered an opinion to anyone, and I didn't involve myself in other people's business. My embrace of technology consisted only of a telephone, and I had no desire to ever watch television or utilize any facet of social media. As a result, my thoughts and my life remained private, allowing me to live without much influence or objection from outsiders.

Keeping my mind occupied was important to my mental health, and my entertainment came from watching people, reading, and above all, surfing. For me, surfing was more than a leisure activity or sport; it had become part of who I was. It kept me alive, and allowed me to focus on being instead of doing. It was my belief that my continued existence was reliant upon surfing as much as it was anything else.

No two waves were ever alike, and each day of surfing was an experience different than the last. Although waiting for a wave allowed my mind to wander, often leaving me with thoughts of activities or events well beyond my grasp, paddling for a wave filled me with hope, and finally catching a wave was one thing and one thing only.

Cleansing.

FUCK BUDDY

Cleansing to my mind, spirit, and soul.

Scrubbing my mind of the lingering sexual desires that seemed to so freely inhabit it was much more than something I hoped for, it was a necessity. Without surfing, I had little doubt I would be able to exist amongst the masses of inhabitants in the state I so proudly called home. Surfing allowed me to live a life between each wave I caught, one with minimal desire to do anything else but catch the next wave.

Summer was now in full swing, and although Liv and I often ate dinner at her home, we had been doing so more frequently since she swore off dating. I enjoyed our meals together, and always looked forward the odd conversations we had.

I peered across the table and admired her choice of clothing. Shorts, flats, and a tasteful turquoise tank were a simple choice, but seeing her arms exposed satisfied me greatly. She told her stories with her hands, tossing them about as she spoke, and I enjoyed watching her lean muscular arms as she did so.

"Being single sucks," she said.

It seemed I ate a Liv's home more frequently than my own. If it wasn't for her, I would probably be forced to survive on fruit, vegetables, yogurt, and cottage cheese.

"So how long has it been?" I asked.

I watched intently as she silently finished cutting a piece of chicken, picked it up with her fork, and let the utensil dangle loosely from her fingertips as she gazed beyond me for a moment.

She grinned. "Three months, four days, and roughly twenty hours."

Liv's recent anti-dating stage initially left her with a large hole in her schedule. After a few days of sulking, she filled the void by spending all of her free time with me. I found it hard to believe three months had passed, but time often seemed to slip away from me without so much as being noticed.

I tried to contain myself, but laughed regardless. "You sound like a recovering alcoholic, not a single woman."

She shrugged and bit half of the piece of chicken from the tip of her fork. I thought of the night I had received the drunken text messages from her, and what had transpired in my life since then. It truly seemed that it had only been a matter of weeks since it happened.

My mind wandered to the time we had spent together since her swearing off of internet dating. "Hard to believe it's been that long. It seems like, I don't know, maybe a few weeks have passed."

I attempted to convert the meals we shared into the amount of weeks that had passed and eventually gave up. "You know, I think one of these days I'm going to look up, and *poof*! Life's going be over with."

She wrinkled her nose and stuck her chin out slightly as she stared at me with eyes of disbelief. "Why do you say that?"

"I don't pay much attention to time," I responded.

"You don't have to." She waved her hand in my direction as she spoke. "The entire world does, but you don't. You surf, you sleep, you surf, you sleep. You probably don't even know what day of the week it is."

I agreed with her completely. I didn't know, and not only did I not know, I really didn't care what day of the week it was.

"I'm not interested in having my life or the events in my life dependent on a clock. *Go to work at this time, come home at that time, it's time to eat, it's time to get up, I have to run to a meeting at 11:45.* I don't know how people do it."

Liv had been my best – and only – friend since we were in fourth grade. According to her, we had been best friends since kindergarten, but I didn't completely agree. My first few years in school were difficult, and even though it seemed everyone wanted to befriend me, I had very little interest in becoming friends with anyone. By the time I was nine years old, I realized to survive I may not need to be friends with everyone, but I certainly needed to be friends with someone.

Liv became that someone.

I picked up a slice of avocado only to have it slip from my fingers when it was half-way to my mouth.

"I envy you," she said.

"Because I don't wear a watch?"

"No, because you don't have a schedule," she said. "And you should use a fork."

I reached for the salt, sprinkled a little onto the avocado and picked it up. "I couldn't live like that. And you doing so is by choice, and nothing more."

"You don't have to pay rent, and I do. Big difference, Dude."

"We've been over this, Liv. You could do what you do from home. Independently you could probably make more money, certainly have more freedom, and be happier. It's your own fault."

She lowered her fork to her plate and sighed. "I don't know. I think it's the risk, it scares me."

"Don't complain, then," I said flatly.

"I can complain if I want."

I widened my eyes. "You shouldn't. You have the capacity to change it, and you choose not to take the risk. Complaining only brings disappointment into your life. Why be disappointed if you don't have to be?"

"You make me mad," she said.

"Okay, be mad. Mad, and reliant upon others to sustain life. Oh, and single by choice."

"That's another thing."

"What's that?"

She placed her fork to the side and reached for her glass of wine. "The single thing. I hate it. It's driving me insane, but I deleted all the apps off my phone and I swore I wouldn't do it anymore. I mean, it *really* sucks. I swear, I have no idea how you do it," she said over the top of her glass.

As she took a drink of wine, I finished chewing my chicken and considered my response. My being single was no doubt a choice, but it was also something I viewed as a necessity. I fully realized a long-term relationship with anyone would be an impossibility, and therefore chose to live a life of solitude.

"I guess it depends on exactly what it is you're after," I said. "You're not going to find the man you'll marry on Tinder, okcupid, or e-fucking-harmony, so why waste your time? Or their time for that matter?"

She took another drink of wine and shook her head. "You aren't listening, I said I didn't know how *you* do it. How you can be single and happy for like *ever*. I'm going insane, and it's only been three months. And, it really doesn't matter if it's my future husband or just some dude to bone, both are human contact and sexual interaction."

I coughed out a laugh and almost choked on my chicken. After taking a drink, I leaned forward, rested my forearms against the table, and gazed at her. Liv was beyond what anyone could describe as beautiful, and in all honesty she could have her pick of the entire single population of the city if someone took the time to get to know her. Her problem, at least in my opinion, was that she didn't perceive herself as valuable.

To be willing to sexually give herself to a man she really didn't know – under the feeble impression she *did* know him because she read whatever he chose to include in his online profile – spoke volumes of her emotional evaluation of herself. In summary, she was far too willing to attach herself to almost anyone who would pay her a moment's notice.

"And, that is exactly what the men on those websites want. Sexual interaction. Nothing more, and there's no way they'll settle for anything less. They're on there to get fucked," I said.

Her mouth fell open and she stared back at me. "How can you say that?"

"Seriously?"

Her disbelief caught me off guard. I glared at her for a moment, pushed myself away from the table, and leaned against the back of my chair. To think she believed the men on the online dating sites were after anything other than sex was laughable. I realized I should address the topic cautiously, but also felt a need to make sure she understood my true thoughts.

"You know, when you started doing that a few years ago, I gave you my opinion, and it sure hasn't changed since. Most of the guys lurk on those sites are looking for someone to fuck, and after they get it they go home to their girlfriend or wife. After a few weeks or a month, they make an excuse to *break up*, and then move on to another victim. They're a bunch of narcissists feeding their self-esteem by their own personal count of the women they bone," I said.

She gave me a *pffft*, and reached for her wine. "You don't know that."

"You're right, I don't. Answer me this, how many dates have you gone on since you started?"

She swallowed her wine, cast her eyes toward the kitchen cabinets, and stared blankly for a while. "Like, since the beginning?"

"Yes, Liv, the beginning."

"I don't know, maybe fifty."

I leaned forward and rested my elbows on the table as I nodded in agreement. "Fifty. I'd say that's pretty accurate. Probably one a month give or take, for four years."

She took another sip of wine and wagged her eyebrows playfully.

"Now, how many twenty-five-year-old women in this city do you think have been on fifty dates in four years?" I asked.

She lowered her eyes to her plate and seemed consumed by the question. My guess was that she was going through her short list of girlfriends, and was truly trying to count the dates she knew they had been on in the amount of time we had been out of school. After a long silent pause, she glanced up.

"None?"

I nodded. "I'll agree. None. I'd say most of them, if they're single, have been on two or possibly three a year."

"You *always* do this," she snapped as she leaned away from the table.

I chuckled. "What?"

"Change the subject," she said. "I asked you about you, and you turned it into me. I asked how *you* stay single, and you didn't answer. You never answer. You just say you're satisfied or whatever. Why don't you answer me?"

She reached for her wine, finished what was in the glass, and stood from her seat. In a half-drunken stumbling maneuver, she stepped to the counter, grabbed the bottle of wine, and pulled the cork.

"More?" she asked, holding the bottle at arm's length.

I laughed to myself about her drunken behavior. She didn't get drunk often, but when she did, she was generally pretty cute.

"I'm good."

She poured her glass as full as she was able and sat down. "So, you're single and I'm single. I think you could have any girl you wanted, and you tell me I could have any guy I wanted. We're both going without, and it's fucking ridiculous."

I shrugged and glanced down at my plate. I was no longer interested in eating, but felt a need to since she had taken the time to prepare it. As I considered taking another bite of chicken, she cleared her throat loudly.

I glanced in her direction.

She tossed her head back, flipped her hair over her shoulders, and pressed her biceps into the sides of her breasts. "I swear, we should just date each other," she said with a laugh.

I pried my eyes from her bulging breasts, dropped my gaze to my plate, and cut a slice off the end of the chicken breast. Although throughout the course of our entire friendship we had never discussed it, I couldn't say the thought of fucking Liv hadn't crossed my mind. In fact, I had spent some time while waiting on a wave doing just that – thinking of fucking her. Dating her, however, was out of the question. I had no desire to be in a relationship with her and chance losing my only friend when the relationship went to hell, and there was no doubt in my mind that it would go straight to hell at some point.

I poked the tines of the fork into the piece of chicken and hesitated for a few seconds, hoping she would change the topic of conversation.

My efforts to act as if I heard nothing, however, didn't last long enough for me to raise the fork to my mouth.

She cleared her throat again. "So, are you going to just keep doing that?"

"Doing what?"

"Acting like you didn't hear me."

"You've had too much to drink."

"One glass or three glasses, we'd be having the same conversation, Luke. I'm twenty-five, and I'm sick of it. I know we have each other, and I love this. You know, our friendship." She waved her hand back and forth between us. "But I need some dick."

I did my best to act preoccupied with the chicken. It seemed to do nothing short of urge her to press even further. As I reached for my fork, she continued.

She lifted her glass of wine. "No matter how you want to look at it, this is the first time in four years that I've been single."

I chewed the piece of cold meat and poked at the remaining chicken breast with the tip of the fork. She was right, but I really didn't want to think about it. I wanted her to change the subject. Knowing her as well as I did, however, I realized she probably had no intention of doing so. There would never be a woman on earth with the natural ability to please me more than Liv, but finding a woman – any woman – to be able to fulfill my sexual desires would be close to impossible.

"Well, you know, not *actively* looking for someone to date," she said. "And, the more I think about it, it's the only time since you've been single that I *wasn't* dating. So what do you think about that?"

I peered over the table and tried to purse my lips. Instead, my mouth twisted into a smirk as I spoke. "About what?"

"I swear. You're Mister evasive. I know after Valerie you said you were done, but there's no way you're done. Not like *done*."

When Valerie and I broke up, I swore I'd never be in another relationship, and I hadn't so much as kissed a girl since. Convinced the possibility of me being compatible with a woman was zero, I saw no future in even trying.

"I'm thinking we should…I don't know…maybe try and…"

"Try and what, Liv?"

"I don't know. I was just thinking. I mean, we're best friends and we never argue about anything. And, well…I mean…"

I had spent all of my days since my one and only relationship ended trying to rid my mind of thoughts of sex, and of women for that matter. As attracted as I was to Liv, dating her was out of the question.

The thought of having sex with her, however, was something I struggled with as I waited for each and every wave.

But I wasn't satisfied with simply having sex.

When it came to sex, there was something wrong with me. Terribly wrong. Attempting to fulfill my sexual desires ended my first relationship, and I was quite certain it would end any relationship I had in the future. If Liv really wanted to date, she would have an expectation of sex. If we took our relationship along that path, it would inevitably end and end quickly.

I had no interest in losing my only friend.

I stared down at my plate, wondering if she was speaking out of sexual frustration and had no intention of acting upon her statement, or if she was half-drunk and being somewhat truthful. It was also quite possible she was suggesting we attempt nothing other than being more active friends, and begin going out on *dates*, but remain friends.

Thinking of the possibilities caused me to feel as if the temperature in the kitchen had increased thirty degrees. I wiped my brow with the back of my hand, glanced up, and studied her.

She sat in her chair with the stem of the wine glass dangling between her thumb and middle finger. With her long brown hair pulled up into a bun and her eyes clearly indicating the effects of the three glasses of wine, she looked remarkable.

She always looked remarkable.

"We can't date, Liv. It's out of the question," I said flatly.

Her idea of dating was entertaining to think about, but it wouldn't work. We were adults. Adults who dated eventually ended up having sex, and sex, at least for us, would end the relationship. Considering my sexual hang-ups, to agree to date her would be to cast our friendship aside. I wasn't of the opinion my sexual preferences were wrong, but I was convinced they weren't widely accepted.

She attempted to raise her glass and sloshed a portion of the wine onto the table in front of her. After her eyes fell to the spill, she raised them to meet mine and grinned. "Because?"

"Because I can't risk losing you."

She licked the wine from her lips. "Is that the only reason?"

It wasn't, but for the sake of the conversation we were having, I didn't need to expand my response to include my sexual deviance.

"Yes," I lied.

"Fine." She placed her glass of wine to the side and leaned forward. As she fixed her hypnotic green eyes on mine, she continued. "Forget dating. Forget a relationship. Let's remain friends. I agree, losing you is something I can't chance. But, I'm fucking dying."

"How so?"

"I need some dick. I really do. You're single, I'm single. I think we should just start fucking. You know, be fuck buddies. What do you think about that? You and me being fuck buddies?"

I sat and stared with my mouth agape, mentally prepared to provide her with a long list of reasons why we couldn't be friends and have sex with each other.

Instead, I gawked at her as if she had just found a way to cure cancer.

She leaned away from the table and picked up her glass of wine. Her eyes widened as she raised it to her mouth. "Well, at least you're thinking about it."

She was right.

I was thinking about it.

And, although I knew it probably should have, it didn't sound like a bad idea.

Not bad at all.

CHAPTER THREE

LIV

After being friends for two-and-a-half decades and never once discussing it, I found it hard to believe we had reached a point where not only were we talking about sex, but seriously considering becoming sexually active with each other. It was now two weeks after my suggestion of becoming fuck buddies, and we sat in the living room discussing it at length. It was the third time we talked about it, but this time seemed to be more serious. After discussions of sexually transmitted diseases and me reminding him I was on birth control, the conversation migrated to the sex act itself. Luke claimed to be some kind of sexual deviant, but as far as I was concerned, his personal diagnosis of what he perceived as a fault was just one more reason for us to be fucking each other.

"Sex is sex. I mean, really. Nothing against you, but I don't see how it's going to be much different," I said.

He gazed down at the floor for a moment and appeared to be in deep thought. I mentally stood firm in my opinion that his warnings of my inability to accept his sexual offerings were unwarranted.

"So, I guess surfing is surfing." He turned to face me. "You've seen me surf, right?"

"Uhh. Yeah."

To see Luke surf was much different than watching anyone else attempt to do so. Typically, rows upon rows of surfers would wait for the waves, paddling to catch each and every one. Most failed completely at catching anything. Luke, on the other hand, waited for the perfect wave, and appeared to always catch it right before it broke, riding it in a manner that made it seem like he was personally taming it from a thirty-foot tall treacherous beast to the flattened white foam that softly washed to the shore.

He cocked one eyebrow. "Can you compare my surfing to all surfing?"

I shook my head. "No. Not at all."

"Remember when we were in high school, and you came to see me compete for my black belt?"

"Sure."

"How many matches did you watch before it was my turn?"

I shrugged and tried to remember the competition. "I don't know, like, maybe, eight or ten."

"Did any of them seem as talented as me?"

I shook my head. I couldn't say I agreed with his theory that I would recede into a ball of emotion and sit in the corner babbling, but he was making some very valid points regarding the difference in his abilities as they compared to everyone else's.

"You made your point. But that doesn't mean I'm going to be an emotional wreck over this. You said you weren't abusive, and that you weren't into that sado-whatever-shit, so I think I'm good to go," I said.

He brushed his hair from his face and laughed. "Good to go, huh?"

"Yep."

His eyes fell to my waist and slowly rose the length of my torso, stopping as they met mine. "And, to clarify, I said I wasn't into violence and that I didn't have sadistic tendencies. But, our opinions of what's sadistic may differ. I've taken a long look at myself, and I'm a sadist, by definition. I obtain satisfaction from not only being in charge, but from watching my partner suffer. Mentally suffer."

I chuckled.

He stared at me without an ounce of emotion.

"Listen. I'm sure some women let guys fuck them because they feel obligated. I've told you before. But just in case you forgot. I like dick." I assured him.

His expression didn't change.

"Actually," I said with a smile. "I *love* it."

His mouth twisted into smirk and he shook his head in apparent disbelief.

"So, what are we down to? Mental sexual suffering? Yeah, I think I'll be fine," I said, hoping to convince him I was no newcomer to being mind-fucked by men.

"That simple, huh?" He chuckled.

It didn't sound so bad at first, but I was beginning to wonder. "Well, what are you talking about? Mental suffering? From sex?"

"I don't know how to explain it. I just like seeing you get confused and nervous about sex. The mental struggle with continuing or whatever. When you want to continue, but you don't. I don't know," he said, shaking his head as he spoke.

It sounded pretty ridiculous to me. "Sounds good to me. I'm still thinking I'm good to go."

As his gaze fell to the floor and he continued to shake his head, my pussy began to tingle. I found the thought of it all very intriguing, but beyond that, I was becoming aroused thinking of just what mental suffering would or even could come from having sex. My mind eventually drifted to thoughts of Luke fucking me into a babbling pile of naked flesh, and it was there that I remained until he snapped his fingers and brought me out of my sexual slumber.

"Where the hell did you go?" he asked.

I squinted and stared. "Huh?"

"You faded away or something. I was talking, and you were just sitting there slobbering," he said with a laugh.

I wiped the sides of my mouth with the back of my hand and gazed down at what appeared to be very dry skin. "I wasn't slobbering."

"Well, you were pretty close."

"What did you say?" I asked.

He waved his hand in my direction. "Forget it."

"No, no, no. No, don't start that *forget it* shit. What?" I snapped back.

"Everyone's a gangster until someone pulls a gun," he said.

"What the fuck does that mean?"

"It means when shit gets real I guess you'll find out if you're *good to go*."

I laughed. It sounded ridiculous. "When the shit gets real? Are we talking about rescuing hostages or fucking?"

"Making slow passionate love isn't something I'm interested in," he said. "It might get rough or even be mentally exhausting, but one thing it won't be is easy."

Point taken, but I'm not like a normal woman. I like dick.

A lot of it.

I twisted my mouth to the side and widened my eyes slightly. It was my best *is that all you've got* look. He's seen it a million times if he'd seen it once.

He lowered his head and chuckled. "Fuck buddies, huh? I guess we can agree to give it a try. But if we do, you just need to remember, I like weird shit."

Weird rough sex?

Yeah, count me in.

I sat at one end of the couch and he at the far other. I peered toward him as he babbled his rhetoric, trying to assure myself if we took this step that I would be just fine. It was just sex, at least that's what I kept telling myself. I was convinced some women had sex for the sole purpose of satisfying their partner or to keep the relationship from falling apart. Others, and probably a rather small portion of the general population, truly enjoyed it. I was one of the rare few that loved sex and everything about it.

As I admired him with what seemed to be a different set of eyes than I had ever viewed him through, I decided not only was I *good to go* as far as sex went, but that I was ready.

Ready for him to try and fuck me to death.

Or at least into a pile of babbling flesh.

I stood up. "Yeah. I'm good to go."

His eyes followed me as I stood. Quickly, his face washed with confusion.

I placed my hands on my hips and forced a sigh. "I mean we're both adults. We've been friends for as long as we can remember. I'm not going to let anything get between us. If we're just going to remain friends and bring sex into the friendship, it's not that big of a deal. If having sex with you turns me into a wreck, or I can't handle it, we'll stop. But, let me just warn you of something before we go any further."

"What's that?" he asked.

I cocked my hip to the side and did my best to mentally undress him. "I just might fuck *you* into a pile of babbling flesh. That's what you said, right? Babbling flesh? I was going to be sitting in the corner babbling to myself, that's what you said. Well, get ready to babble, Mister."

He pressed his hands into the cushion of the couch and straightened his posture. Slowly, and without speaking, he stood and turned to face me. He brushed his hair from his face, gazed at me with his thin brown eyes, and moved toward me with an air of confidence.

I stood, frozen in place.

He leaned into me, brushing his cheek along mine lightly until his mouth was against my left ear. My shoulders instinctively raised. Goosebumps formed along my arms. With his warm breath in my ear, I stood there attempting to act unaffected by his approach. Nothing could have been further from the truth. I wanted him to show me just what it was that would wad me into a ball of blubbering flesh, but part of me was afraid.

"Liv, you're shaking," he whispered.

A chill ran along my spine. I swallowed heavily, knowing a response was impossible.

As he pulled away from me, his lips parted slightly. I desperately wanted him to kiss me. Halfway between being scared to death and too damned excited to move, I stood and watched his each and every movement as if there was nothing I could do to either join him or prevent him from proceeding. It was something I had spent many drunken evenings thinking about and hoping for, but had always dismissed as nothing more than just that.

Hope.

I stood silently as he moved closer. I waited. I wanted. But more than anything, I wondered. I knew whatever Luke offered me would be enjoyable from a sexual standpoint, but I doubted I was truly prepared. If his ability to fuck me was equal to his ability to surf or fight, I was going to be in trouble. As his chest pressed lightly against mine I closed my eyes and hoped my shaking legs would continue to hold me up.

I could feel his warm breath against my mouth. Eager, I opened my eyes.

He leaned his head to the side at the last moment, brushing his lips lightly past mine. As he pressed his jaw against the side of my face and exhaled lightly against my ear my panties all but burst into flames.

"Take off your shorts, Liv," he breathed.

An ever so slight tingling in my pussy assured me it was alright to proceed. My hands fell to the waist of my shorts and I fumbled to unfasten the button. A simple task that I did no less than half a dozen times a day all of a sudden became impossible. After finally unbuttoning the shorts, I forced my thumbs underneath my panties and began to press them down my legs.

He didn't tell me to take off my panties.

For whatever nervous reasons, I wondered if he was testing me.

I released my panties and pushed my shorts down along my thighs until they fell to the floor. With my underwear now riding low on my hips, I stood up and kicked my shorts to the side.

Gracefully, he knelt in front of me. I bit into my bottom lip and watched as he traced his fingers along the top edge of my panties, softly pressing them against my skin from the center of my stomach toward each hip. My eyes fell closed as I felt his fingers slide underneath the bottom lace and follow the fabric until the tips of his fingers rested against the sides of my pussy. As he carefully caressed the skin on the inside of my upper thighs with his thumbs, I released my lip and drew in a sharp unexpected breath.

I was absolutely soaked.

He pulled my panties to the side and I felt his warm breath against my wetness. My eyes shot open and I gasped as his mouth pressed against my swollen mound. With precision, he flicked his tongue against my clit ever so gently. As I embraced the feeling of his tongue teasing me with precision, he pulled away and gazed up at me.

I stood there, trembling, incapable of much more than returning his gaze. My lips parted slightly in anticipation as he reached for the bottom of his shirt and pulled it over his head. As many times as I had seen Luke shirtless at the beach, nothing could have prepared me to see him half-naked and on his knees with his face hovering in front of my wanting pussy.

I gazed down at him filled with wonder. Why, I thought, had we taken so long to decide to give this a try? He reached around me, dug his fingertips into the cheeks of my ass, and pulled me into his face. Again, he encompassed me fully with his lips. I let out an unexpected moan as his tongue began to circle my swollen clit.

Rhythmically, I bucked my hips against his face, fucking his mouth as he carefully flicked my clit with the tip of his tongue.

Quickly, I felt myself begin to peak and closed my eyes. As my moaning rang out into the room, a deep groan escaped his lips and transferred into my wet flesh in mild vibrations. His lips and tongue continued to nibble and work their magic on my nub until a tingling filled me and I bellowed out into the room.

The intensity of the orgasm was unlike anything I had ever

experienced. I pulled my hips away from his face and peered down at him, only to see him gazing up, his face covered with my wetness.

Slowly, he stood.

Our lips met. I closed my eyes and allowed myself to become lost in the moment. His tongue danced with mine magically, and along with it came the taste of my orgasm. As we kissed he pulled me firmly against him. With my head spinning and my mind trying to make sense of the situation I had so quickly agreed to become a part of, I kissed him eagerly in return, savoring each and every movement of his lips and tongue. He dragged his nails along my back as he pressed his palms deep against my muscles, his hands coming to a stop at my waist. As I ground my hips against his, I felt his rigid shaft against my leg.

I pulled my mouth from his and slowly shifted my eyes from his broad chest along his chiseled abdomen and eventually to his waist.

Without speaking, he reached down, untied his shorts, and pushed them to the floor.

A pronounced "V" shape in his lower stomach muscles commanded my focus to fall further, following the "V" to the area it so clearly pointed to. I stared, all but paralyzed by the sight of what was the most beautiful cock I had ever seen. As my mind drifted to thoughts of being filled with something so perfectly shaped, I couldn't help but wonder if the girth of his third leg would tear me apart.

An unwanted sigh escaped my lungs. With my focus fixed on his thickness, I reached for the bottom of my shirt. I pulled it over my head and reached behind my back. As I awkwardly fumbled with the clasp of my bra, he began to slowly stroke his shaft with his right hand.

With my eyes glued to his insanely large and ever-so-stiff dick, I dropped my bra to the floor. His hand continued to slowly work its way up and down the shaft, all but commanding me to remain focused on the swollen member I had spent so many years fantasizing about. I pushed my panties to the floor.

His free hand gripping my neck startled me. He leaned closer, pressing his bare chest to mine. As we stood with our eyes locked, he slowly rubbed the tip of his swollen cock along my pussy lips.

He stared at me blankly as he pressed the head of his dick against my wet pussy, tapping my clit at the end of each stroke. My heart raced as he tightened his grip on my neck. I had never been choked before, and although I felt some guilt for feeling the way I did, there was something about him doing it that was driving me fucking insane. He studied my eyes through thinning slits, his mouth twisting into a slight smirk with each stroke of his swollen flesh against my wetness.

He released my neck.

I gasped.

"Are you ready?" he asked.

I pursed my lips, swallowed heavily, and nodded.

"I asked you a question, Liv." He cleared his throat. "Are. You. Ready?"

Without thinking, I reached for my neck and rubbed where his hand had been. What felt like small electric shocks tingled deep within my pussy. He stood before me, stroking his cock as he waited for an answer. Luke. My best friend. My best friend with added benefits.

What the fuck did I get myself into?

I wasn't ready.

I released my neck and lowered my hand. "Yes."

I had no idea of what he was going to do, but I knew I wanted him to do something. I had a crush on Luke since we were young, and had spent many hours fantasizing about being with him sexually. Having him stand before me naked had me more excited than I ever would have imagined. As I stood there in the heightened state of sexual bliss, deep in my mind a small bit of fear lingered.

Fear of the unknown.

"Close your eyes," he said flatly.

As much as I didn't want to, I did as he asked. The room fell dark. I stood in the silence filled with wonder, excited, and aroused more than I had ever been in my life.

I felt his arm around my thighs. His other arm pressed against my upper back. His warm breath against my ear.

"I'm going to pick you up," he whispered into my ear.

I pressed my tongue against the roof of my mouth and attempted to swallow. "Okay," escaped my dry lips as a shaky insincere response.

In an instant, I was upside down, dangling over the floor head-first. His hands gripped my waist firmly and lifted me into a position where my legs dangled over his shoulders and my bare torso was against his. I pressed my hands into his thighs and opened my eyes. His stiff cock twitched in front of my face.

He buried his tongue deep into my pussy, and I arched my back, breathing a moan of pleasure into the room. After a few seconds, I relaxed and I wrapped my lips around his twitching shaft. Slowly, I began to work my mouth along the length of his cock. Thrilled to have Luke's stiff dick in my mouth, but even more excited at his ability to lick pussy, I tried my best to focus on what I was doing, not what he was doing. A short moment later, and another intense orgasm shook my body to the core.

For once in his life, Luke was wrong. I *was* ready.

Holding me with my legs over his shoulders and my ass in his face, he continued to tongue-fuck me into a weakened mess. Maybe it was part of his plan, I thought. Quite possibly he planned to lick me into a state of being that allowed him to squash me mentally, causing me to revert back to my status of being single and having no sex whatsoever.

Two intense orgasms later, and he lowered me to the floor. Although half-exhausted from reaching repeated climax and dizzy from being suspended upside down over the floor, I was far from being mentally bankrupt.

With his swollen shaft glistening from my saliva, I sat naked on the floor and watched as he began to slowly stroke it in his hand.

A pile of babbling flesh?

I think not.

Without speaking, he lowered himself to the floor and reached for my hips. After turning me over onto my back, he wrapped his arms under my legs and brought my knees to my chest. My pussy now high in the air for the taking, he did just that.

As I felt the pressure against the inner walls of my vagina, I gasped, uncertain of my ability to accept his massive girth. Slowly, cautiously, and with what appeared to be great care, he worked his hips back and forth. Praying for a little relief, I bit against the inside of my lip and stared at his ripped bronze-colored torso. With each *in* stroke, I drew a quick choppy breath, hoping the next would be slightly more pleasurable. Eventually, he slid deep inside of me, causing me to sigh not only in relief, but in a sense of satisfaction I wasn't sure I had ever felt. With wide eyes I gazed at him, somewhat proud of having accepted his full length. His focus was intense, but he was focused not on me, but on fucking me.

His dark eyes were filled with intensity and determination. Although they looked in my direction, they seemed to peer through me and if not into my soul, certainly well beyond what was on the surface.

"Liv…"

I released my lip from the tight clench of my teeth. "Yes?"

"We're friends. It has to stay that way. No matter what," he said.

It seemed to be a strange time to be having the conversation, but I agreed nonetheless. "Uhhm. Yeah, I agree."

"Ready?" he asked.

For fucking what?

"Sure," I responded, far more interested at the time in fucking than talking.

Nothing could have prepared me.

He raised his hips, pressed his shoulders into the back of my knees, and gave one last command as I felt the length of his shaft escape me.

He nodded toward my crotch. "Watch."

"Okay," I breathed.

Without further warning, he began to pound himself into me, giving me his entire cock with each stroke. My breath escaped my lungs each time his hips slapped against my ass, barking past my lips as a muffled grunt. My one focus, at least initially, was to keep from screaming for him to stop.

By some means of a sexual miracle, a few moments passed without me giving up. Luke's cock was now hitting spots inside of me that I had no idea even existed. He continued to fuck me without reservation, and seemed to be fully determined to turn me into the pile of babbling flesh he had warned me I would become.

Equally determined to succeed at being his sexual punching bag, I closed my eyes and focused on my cock-filled twat. My nostrils flared as I inhaled a hint of his cologne mixed with the aroma of our sex. Convinced I was going to allow him to punish my pussy until he was completely satisfied he had met his sexual match; I did my best to find a happy place for my mind to reside while he continued.

"Watch!" he bellowed.

Shit.

I opened my eyes and gazed beyond his wide chest, past his washboard abdomen, and between my legs. With his muscular torso a blur, I watched as the tightly stretched skin of his glistening dick disappeared stroke after powerful stroke into my wet and quickly becoming sore pussy.

Somehow, he found the energy to increase his pace. More suited for a sexual run and less prepared for an all-out sprint, my head began to feel light and dizzy.

"I love this tight little pussy of yours," he said.

I had so much I wanted to say, but found myself incapable of speaking.

With the top of his shaft punishing my clit as he ground his hips against mine, a tingling sensation ran through me from my swollen nub to my nipples. I inhaled a slow breath, well aware – at least for me – that the end was near.

It was coming.

I sank my teeth into my bottom lip and continued the torturous task of watching him take ownership of my pussy. Even though I repeatedly reminded myself we were no more than friends, I couldn't help but struggle with the fact that I had never been satisfied by a man's cock as much as I was by Luke's.

And I was certain I never would be.

I felt my pussy clench against his throbbing shaft, providing its own *thank you for being here* moment, but the precursor to my climactic exit did little to slow his pace. Contrary to his demands, I closed my eyes and moaned as I reached a level of climax I had never before encountered.

His pace slowed slightly, his cock swelled, and as I gasped for another gulp of air, he erupted inside of me.

Thank God.

My work was done. Not only had I satisfied him to the point of orgasm, but I had done so without turning into a mindless babbling ball of flesh as he suggested I would. Filled with pride, I blinked and wrapped my arms around him.

As he released my legs, I gazed around the room. Quickly, I became confused. We had been fucking on the floor of the living room, and the last I knew, we were at the end of the couch. Now fifteen feet away, closer to my favorite ottoman, I realized there was only one way we could have traveled so far.

Luke had forcefully fucked me across the entire living room floor.

He collapsed onto me, his bare chest pressing against mine. I closed my eyes and listened as his breathing changed from an irregular pattern to a more predictable even pace. Satisfied that I held up to my end of the sexual bargain, I decided remaining mute about the subject wasn't exactly my style.

I had gone the distance with the sexual deviant and I needed to claim my successes.

"I'm afraid the back of my ass might be covered in a few rug burns, but I'm not a babbling pile of flesh, Mister," I said in a sarcastic tone.

He rolled off of me and turned to his side. The corners of his mouth curled into an unapologetic shitty little smile. "Not yet."

"What does that mean?" I snapped back, still beaming with pride from my accomplishments.

"It means what I said. *Not yet*, Liv. You will. I was just seeing if we fit each other."

"And?"

He locked eyes with me. "I'd say we're good to go."

"Did you have your doubts?"

"Not really," he responded.

Fuck yes.

"Me neither," I said.

I rolled to my side, cupped my hand between my legs, and stood. The pain in my shoulders and the top of my butt were all the reminder I needed that I would be covered in rug burns.

As I waddled to the bathroom, I was further reminded of just how big Luke's cock really was.

And I couldn't help but wonder what his *not yet* remark would bring with it when the time came.

CHAPTER FOUR

LUKE

My former girlfriend and I began a relationship at a young age, and it was then that I determined something was wrong with me, sexually speaking, that is. As much as my mind enjoyed the thought of sex, and as pleasing as the mental visions of sex were to me, the act of sex had to either include sadistic thoughts or acts. If for some reason it didn't, I wasn't able to perform.

I had my own theories on why I was the way I was, but I wasn't willing to discuss them with others or attempt to pry deeper into my inner psyche in an effort to resolve issues that were embedded within my being during my childhood.

Embracing who I was and what I enjoyed was much easier, and allowed a no excuses approach to life. I had my reservations, however, on whether or not Liv could accept my sexual desires once they exposed themselves completely.

Five years. It had been five years since I had sex. Liv had no real idea what she was in for, and as much as I loved her as a friend, I had to convince myself with each passing minute that being fuck buddies was the answer to each of our problems. I knew one thing. For it to work, I needed to take matters slow and easy.

Slow and easy wasn't my strength, unless it was during one of my midnight strolls down along the beach. Sex was something I truly enjoyed, but I only seemed to enjoy it if I was wreaking havoc on my sexual partner.

It seemed surreal to be having sex with Liv. For a lifetime I had placed her in a protective bubble, and as much as I shared with her, I didn't share everything. My sexual desires and opinions regarding their origin were things I had always kept to myself. As time passed there was no doubt Liv would become aware of what my sexual desires truly were, and I held onto the hope that when the time came she accepted them. If not, it would be apparent our decision to include sex in our friendship was a poor one.

Either way I would be satisfied, my preference leaning slightly toward maintaining the friendship already in place and somehow adding sex to it without sacrificing anything else. Succeeding at it would be difficult, but I was driven by a challenge.

The challenge before me, however, was a much more difficult one than I had faced in some time. I needed to convince Liv not to buy a pair of sandals it appeared she desperately felt she needed. Being her best friend and fuck buddy was rewarding in many respects, but she definitely had her shortcomings, and shoe shopping was a great reminder.

"Because they're fucking ugly, that's why," I said.

She lifted her foot and gazed down at the sandal. "I think they're cute."

"You think they're cute because they're on sale. How many pairs of sandals do you have in your closet that you've never worn?" I asked, glancing one more time toward the hideous shoe.

"They're only thirty bucks. Marked down from a hundred," she said.

"They're stupid. They've got beads all over the straps, and they're all rectangular and square, and they've got sharp edges. They'll cut your feet to shreds, and they look like shit. They're marked down because no one wanted them. If something has a yellow 'SALE' tag on it, you'll buy it. You can't help it. Your closet is full of unworn shit. I swear. Go ahead, buy 'em. I bet you never wear those ugly fuckers once," I said, waving my hand toward the open box.

Over the years, Liv and I shopped together quite often. I rarely bought anything, only because I needed very little. My wardrobe consisted of a few pairs of jeans, several pullovers, board shorts, shorts, tee shirts, and a handful of shoes – all of which were worn regularly. Liv, on the other hand, purchased whatever was on sale, regardless of her actual need, and the items piled up in her closet like waste at a landfill. No matter what it was, if it had a 'SALE' sticker on it, she had to stop and look at it. Convincing her she didn't need it was difficult, especially if she saw it as a bargain.

Personally, I believed she shopped the way she did to feel better about herself. Her lack of a male companion in her life caused her to feel inadequate and unattractive. In the past, I let her shop without much opposition from me. For some reason, on this particular day, I felt the need to convince her otherwise.

"What's ugly about them?" she asked.

I reached for the shoe still sitting in the box. "Everything."

I held the sandal in my hand and pointed to the sole. What appeared to be a piece of wood was sandwiched between two thin pieces of leather. "Look. The sole is made from a piece of wood and two pieces of leather. It's not even flexible."

She shrugged. "So."

"If this was a sole for a pair of heels, fine. But for a pair of sandals?

You want sandals to be flexible. If they're not, this strap is going to tear your toes up."

"And these beads?" I drug my finger along the beads that covered the toe strap. "They'll make sure your toes are torn to shreds. Fuck, just look at them."

"They're only thirty bucks, and they're cute," she said.

"Give your thirty bucks to that guy on the corner with the harmonica."

The sales clerk walked past, and as she did, she turned toward us and grinned. I raised my hand to get her attention. "Ma'am, we have some questions."

"Luke, don't," Liv warned.

She stepped to my side, glanced at Liv and shifted her eyes to me. "How can I help you?"

I held the shoe in front of me and smiled. "Why are these shoes on sale?"

"Excuse me?"

"These shoes. Why are they on sale? The season isn't over, so why are they on sale? Is there something wrong with them?"

"Oh, no. We're overstocked," she said with a smile and a nod.

"See?" Liv said mockingly.

I glanced around the store. No less than two hundred different pairs of shoes were displayed. I glanced at the sale rack behind Liv. Eight pairs of shoes were on sale.

I met her gaze. "Overstocked?"

She nodded and grinned. "Yes."

"So, when you get shoes in, *new* shoes, do you receive random shipments? Like a hundred pairs of this kind, and fifteen pairs of another? Or do you get roughly the same quantity of each pair?"

She scrunched her nose. "What do you mean?"

"Simple question. When you receive shoes, do you get the same number of pairs of each shoe, roughly?"

She tilted her head to the side and stared as if I was asking trade secrets of the industry.

"I suppose so," she said.

I tossed the sandal into the box. As I turned toward the sales clerk, I continued. "So if you're overstocked, it can only be because no one bought this shoe. The shoes that sell well aren't here on the sale rack, right?"

"We typically sell out pretty quickly of the good shoes," she said.

I glanced at Liv and grinned. "The good ones?"

"I meant the good selling ones," she said. "Any other questions?"

"Average women's shoe size?" I asked.

She smiled. "Eight is the new seven. Size eight."

"Anything else?"

"No, I think that's it."

She turned and walked away. I gazed blankly out the storefront windows toward the *Sephora* across the street. I didn't need to ask Liv what size shoe she wore, I had bought her enough shoes for Christmas and birthdays that I knew, but I turned to her and asked anyway.

"What size is your foot, Liv?"

She tossed the sandal in the box. "You know it's an eight."

"Well, if they're not even sold out of the most common size, that can only mean one thing, no one is buying them."

"Well, crap." She glanced toward the sale rack. "I don't like any of the others."

"Do you need another pair of fucking sandals?"

"If they're 75% off? Yeah."

I shook my head. She had no less than thirty pairs of shoes in her closet that were still in boxes, and had yet to be worn. Loose in her closet and scattered about her home she had to have another one hundred pair if she had one. She needed another pair of shoes like I needed another fucking surfboard.

I turned toward the door. "Come on. Let's go across the street."

"What's across the street?"

"Sephora," I said. "Let's go spend that thirty bucks on makeup."

"Are you saying I need new makeup? Do I look bad?" she asked as she fumbled to put her shoe on.

She shifted her eyes to the floor.

"No, you look fabulous."

Liv was many things. She was funny, caring, kind, giving, trustworthy, responsible, and passionate about what she believed in. But, above all, Liv was beautiful. Her beauty was so deeply engrained that it was easily overlooked by passersby, but not by me. Most people didn't realize just how beautiful she was until they took time to try and find a fault in her appearance. By the time they found nothing, they realized she was a remarkably attractive woman.

Her level of humility allowed her to be attractive without effort or even the knowledge that her beauty existed.

Still standing there with her eyes fixed on the floor in front of her, she seemed sad. I lifted her chin with my index finger until her gaze met mine. "You always look fabulous. You're beautiful, Liv. I was thinking maybe one of the artists could show you something they have to help accentuate your natural beauty. Let's go over and just look around."

She beamed with pride and her mouth curled into a smile. "That might be fun."

"I tell you what," I said. "We go over there and you buy some new makeup, and when we get back to your place, I'll make you sit in the corner and babble to yourself. How's that?"

She grinned until her upper lip thinned so much it revealed her teeth. "Sounds like we're going to Sephora."

The makeup would make her feel better about herself. Making her a babbling mess would satisfy me greatly, and hopefully the satisfaction would last for some time.

In my mind the trade was a win-win.

Time, however, would tell if she agreed.

CHAPTER FIVE

LIV

"That just seems weird," I said.

"I told you it was going to get weird quick," he said.

"And I have to stay on the phone the entire time, no matter what?"

"That's right."

"I mean, I can do it, but it just…" I paused and studied him, wondering if he was just fucking with me.

He stared back at me stone-faced. Apparently, he wasn't joking.

"Fine," I said as if the challenge was no big deal. "I'll get my phone."

Luke said he wanted to fuck me, but the entire time we were having sex, I had to be on the phone with one of my friends. He further explained if the conversation ended, he would stop fucking me. He had warned me the sex was going to *get weird quick*, and he was right. But, as crazy as it sounded at first, as I walked toward my purse I got wet just thinking about it. By the time I got back to where he was standing, I was soaked.

I quickly decided being shoved full of Luke's cock while talking to my friend on the phone was much better than getting no dick at all.

"Okay, here's what I was thinking. I'm going to text some people, see who has time to talk, and then I'll make the call. How's that sound?"

He shrugged. "Sounds reasonable."

"I think it sounds genius," I said.

He reached down and tapped his index finger against the very prominent outline the head of his dick was making against the leg of his shorts. "Well, get to it. Thinking about it is making my cock stiff."

I fumbled with my phone and sent out four text messages to girls I hadn't talked to in what seemed like forever. After a few returned texts, Chloe agreed to talk. I couldn't have asked for a better person to talk to, because if push came to shove and she found out what was happening, I knew she might understand.

Chloe was a slut.

"Okay, I've got someone," I said excitedly.

"Call her and put it on speaker," he said.

"On speaker?"

"Do you really think you're going to be able to hold the phone against your ear the entire time?"

"Good point."

I stared down at my phone and inhaled a shallow breath. As long as Luke and I had been friends, I had no idea he was such a sexual weirdo. Now that I knew, I was afraid I still didn't *know*, and wondered as time passed just how weird things might get. He said he was going to ease into the kinky stuff, and my imagination began to run wild with things he may require of me in the future.

"Ready?" I asked.

He wagged his finger in the air. "Better get undressed first."

I bobbed my head side to side mockingly, causing him to grin. After getting fully undressed and wondering why he hadn't done the same, he pointed to my phone.

"Put it on the counter for now," he said.

For now?

"Okay," I said.

I turned toward the kitchen counter, set my phone down, and pressed the button to call her. After a few rings, she answered. Partially just to be a smart-ass, but also to let him know I was ready for whatever he thought he needed to do, I bent at my waist, rested my elbows on either side of the phone, and hiked my ass in the air as high as I could.

"What's up?"

I stared blankly at the phone. It was apparent in my excitement to get started I had called her before I was really prepared to talk. After mentally fumbling with a topic of conversation for a few seconds, I just blurted something out.

"Are you and Mark still dating?" I asked.

"No, I haven't seen him in, I don't know, like a year. Seriously? Has it been that long since we talked?"

"I guess."

"So what's been going on?"

"Well, I tried the dating online thing, and it was awful."

I felt the tip of Luke's cock against my inner thigh. I glanced over my shoulder. Standing behind me, he pulled his shirt over his head and tossed it on the floor beside his shorts. I did my best to mentally prepare for…

Oh Jesus.

I grunted as Luke shoved me full of dick.

"Are you okay?"

"Yeah," I said in a muffled groan. "I just bumped into the counter."

He began to slowly fuck me from behind, but it wasn't anything I couldn't handle while talking on the phone.

"Ouch. I hate it when that happens. Well, yeah. Like on what? Match

dot com or whatever?"

He increased his pace slightly. I pressed my forearms into the counter and sighed. As I exhaled, he shoved himself balls deep into me and held it. The tip of his dick bottomed out and I lunged forward, exhaling again, but this time slightly heavier than before.

"Hello?"

Lost in the feeling of having Luke fuck me again, I had completely forgotten what was going on.

Oh fuck.

"Yeah, sorry. I was thinking. Uhhm. Tinder. I was on Tinder for a while."

I sighed lightly at the sheer joy of having his cock inside of me.

"Sarah had really bad luck on there. All she got was a bunch of creeps."

He began to powerfuck me, pounding himself as deep as he could and pressing my hips into the edge of the countertop with each thrust of his hips.

"Me…too…" I grunted.

The sound of his hips slapping against my ass echoed throughout the kitchen.

"Am I on speaker?"

"Yeah," I breathed. "Cooking. Hands. Are covered. In stuff."

He continued to pound away, his balls banging against my clit with each powerful stroke. The sheer size of his thick shaft stretched my pussy to a new limit, and as painful as it was at first, it was a pain I was now enjoying. I closed my eyes and bit into the inside of my lower lip. Whoever said *size doesn't matter* had never been fucked by a cock the size of Luke's.

Size was *everything*.

Size was the difference between simply getting off and having a mind-blowing orgasm.

Now that I had been filled with Luke's cock and experienced a life altering degree of climax, I realized I was ruined for anyone in the future who had an average-sized dick. If Luke ever stopped fucking me, any future prospects would have to show me the size of their package before I would even agree to let them buy me a drink.

"What's all that noise?"

"There's. A lot. Going. On right. Now."

"I can call you back if you're busy."

"No!" I bellowed.

If she hung up, it was all going to end. I calmed myself, inhaled a shallow breath, and continued. "No, I just…"

His pace slowed considerably.

"Sorry, I just had a bad experience on Tinder and I wanted to tell you about it," I managed to say.

He continued to fuck me ever-so-slowly.

"Oh my God. What happened?"

He pulled out completely. I glanced over my shoulder. He grinned and sauntered around the end of the counter, his stiff cock bouncing up and down with each step. I followed him with narrow eyes, slightly intrigued by what he might be planning. After walking to the opposite edge of the counter, he hopped onto it, got on his knees, and began to inch toward my face.

No. I can't.

There's no way.

With his cock now twitching in front of my face, he opened his mouth wide, pointed to it, and then pointed to my face.

I grinned at the thought of what we were doing, shook my head, and opened my mouth.

He guided the head of his cock past my lips, into my throat, and increased pressure until my gag reflex kicked in. I coughed and gagged against the massive shaft until I was on the verge of passing out, and only then did he pull it from my mouth.

"Hello? Are you okay?"

"Yeah," I coughed. "I choked on my coffee."

"Oh, so what happened on Tinder? Sarah's stories were just creepy."

With tears rolling down my cheeks, I stared down at the phone.

Huh?

I glanced at his saliva covered cock. I would have never guessed it, but I was so turned on my pussy ached. In a brief moment of clarity, I said what I felt might buy me a few minutes of time.

"Tell me what happened to Sarah while I'm stirring this, then I'll tell you my story."

I met his gaze and grinned as I opened my mouth again.

"Okay. So she met this guy, and he was like perfect. He was an architect or something and they started seeing each other, and then they started, you know, having sex. And she was like I think we might even get married or whatever…"

Luke inched his way closer until his cock was pressing against my cheek. I shifted my gaze to the phone. Four minutes and twenty-eight seconds had passed, but it seemed like it had been an hour.

Thwack!

He slapped my face with his cock. I stared back at him, shocked and turned on at the same time.

What the fuck?

He pointed to his mouth.

I opened wide.

He narrowed his eyes and glared as he shoved his cock deep into my throat. My gagging did little to convince him to give me any relief. As the tears ran down my cheeks, he continued to grudge fuck my face.

"...and I was like whatever, bitch, you met his skanky ass on Tinder. But she said he was like this perfect specimen of man. Anyway. So the guy was taking her to the beach, and out to eat and stuff, and they were like going out all the time..."

With my head directly over the phone and Luke's knees straddling it, he continued to fuck my throat not much differently than he fucked my pussy. I never had anyone fuck my face before, and although I would have guessed it was something I wouldn't have enjoyed, something about it was a huge turn-on.

Wide-eyed and with a fire burning between my legs, I glanced up at his muscular chest and down along the rippled muscles of his abdomen. The head of his cock banged against the back of my throat as I hoped Chloe would just keep talking long enough for Luke to finish.

"...so it ends up, this guy is married. And I was like, no shit, bitch. They're all married."

As much as my mind was enjoying the face fucking, my throat continued to reject it. Luke, however, pounded away as Chloe's unrelenting blabbing belched out of the phone's speaker.

"Hello?"

"What's that noise?"

After a few more strokes, he pulled himself from my mouth. I gasped for air and gazed down at the phone. The screen was covered in saliva.

Oh fuck that's hot.

"I…uhhm…I had," I said, trying to catch my breath between words. "I had the same…the uhhm…"

I wiped my mouth and inhaled a choppy breath. "I had the same problem."

Thwack!

He slapped me with his cock again.

"Is this a bad time? I mean it sounds like you've got a lot going on."

I caught my breath, glared at Luke for a moment, and lowered my head toward the phone. "No, I just. No, I'm sorry, I just really wanted to tell you this."

"Okay."

"Sarah's thing? Basically, it happened to me."

Thwack!

I glared at him.

You fucker.

I wiped the saliva from my cheek.

He grinned, brushed the hair out of his face, and climbed down from the countertop.

Thank God.

I realized my best option was to talk fast, tell my story, and get her going on another subject before he started whatever he was going to do.

"So, I met like fifty guys, and they were all dicks. And then I met this guy, just like Sarah, and he was perfect, but the prick was married, and I just lost it. I came home, got drunk, and swore to never use that fucking app again," I blurted.

"That's it?" She laughed. *"That's your story?"*

"Well, yeah. But…" I thought about what to say, and quickly decided to just make something up. "So there was this one guy who wanted me to do this threesome with his roommate, and I was like, are you…"

Luke slowly pushed himself deep inside of me. Not only was it immediately apparent I was ready for him, but my pussy was completely soaked. I opened my mouth wide and exhaled against the screen of the phone as I absorbed the feeling of him filling me with his cock.

Talking on the phone while I was being fucked would have never even entered my mind as an option for sex, but now that I was in the middle of doing it I decided it was the hottest shit I had ever been a part of.

"Hello…"

Oh shit. Come on Liv, you're going to lose her.

"I was like…are you…fucking serious? I didn't know if I was going to get out…of his house alive," I lied. "What was the craziest thing that ever…happened…to…Sarah?"

He pulled half-way out and then shoved himself into me without warning. I coughed out a gasp and all but collapsed chest-first onto the counter. I glanced over my shoulder and glared.

"I don't know. I mean, she was dating guys off there for a while. She finally met someone, but not on there."

He slapped my ass lightly and began to fuck me steadily. With each second or third stroke his hand came down against my butt cheek.

Oh fuck yes. I like that.

I turned, peered over my shoulder, and grinned.

"What are you doing?"

"Cooking," I breathed.

She didn't respond.

Come on, bitch. Tell me something.

For what was probably no more than fifteen or twenty seconds, I let Luke fuck me and slap my ass. My otherwise mundane sex life was at an all-time high, and I was enjoying it. Lost in the sexual act, and completely oblivious to the fact I was going to be deprived of his dick if she hung up, a beep from my low battery warning reminded me of my commitment.

"Uhhm. So, if you're not seeing Mark, who are you seeing?" I rattled the sentence out without so much as taking a breath.

Say something, Chloe. If you ruin this for me, I'll to hate you forever.

The few seconds of phone silence that followed were far from silent on my end.

"This guy. His name is Kavin. With an 'A'. He's kind of a dick, but in a good way. He's really possessive, and kind of controlling, and whatever, but the sex is good."

He began to powerfuck me again without any warning. Whether or not he was withholding cock from me earlier I didn't know, but this time was much different. Each *in* stroke took the breath from me completely, and a muffled *humph* burst from my lungs.

About three or four strokes into it, and my eyes fell closed.

I was going to explode.

Fuck yes, keep fucking me just like that.

Just. Like. That.

As I became engrossed in the sheer joy of Luke fucking me senseless, Chloe's voice caused me to realize it would end and end quickly if I didn't continue to focus not only on being fucked, but on talking to her.

"Hey, Liv, let me call you back, okay?"

I opened my eyes and stared down at my saliva-covered phone.

"Nooooooo!" I groaned.

"Yeah, I really need to go, and you're busy…"

My mind had long since surpassed the confused state, I had been fucked to the point I was delirious. I needed Luke to keep doing exactly what he was doing, and although I sure as fuck didn't need to be talking to Chloe, I realized if I didn't keep her on the phone he would stop. I couldn't think properly, couldn't reason with myself, and damned sure couldn't speak legibly. I needed to focus on what was happening and what I was feeling.

And I was sick of talking on the phone.

"Don't hang up," I begged. "Right now. A guy is fucking me…"

"And. I mean. Like right now. It's. Like a. Sex. Contest," I explained as Luke continued to shove his fat cock into my ever-so-eager pussy.

"And. If I hang up. He's going to. Stop. Just. Stay. Here. Please."

He pounded himself into me even harder. I felt myself begin to reach climax. It was coming, and it was coming fast.

"Stay here on the phone. Until. I. Come," I begged.

"Oh my God, Liv. You're fucking someone? Right now?"

"Uh…huh," I breathed.

"I fucking knew it!"

I closed my eyes and concentrated on Luke's massive cock.

"That's so fucking hot!"

Shut up, bitch.

Luke might have thought I cheated, but I took a big chance in telling her. It worked, and apparently he liked the fact Chloe knew, because he began fucking me like he was trying to kill me. As his balls steadily tapped a rhythmic beat against my clit, I arched my back, craned my neck toward the ceiling, and bellowed out a blood-curdling wail.

Simultaneously, his cock swelled. A few more strokes, and I felt him erupt inside of me. As he came, an orgasm exploded from deep within me, and with it, my entire body was somehow transformed into a sexual bundle of nerves.

The orgasms continued for several seconds, sending electric shocks from the balls of my feet all the way to the back of my skull. Chloe's voice chattered in the background, but I had no idea what she was saying. I opened my eyes and glanced into the kitchen. Everything seemed so out of place and new to me. The few aftershock orgasms that followed caused my legs to shake violently.

I felt Luke pull out and I collapsed onto the counter. My quivering legs struggled to hold me up. Chloe's irritating voice continued to babble from the speaker on the phone.

Exhausted, weak, and incapable of thinking clearly, I simply wanted the feeling to linger as long as it possibly could.

As she continued to vomit her ideas and opinions, I reached for the phone and pressed *end.*

The phone went silent.

I lowered myself to the floor, pulled my knees to my chest, and began to hum.

Size matters.

CHAPTER SIX

LUKE

My home was above my surfboard shop, and the entire building was purchased by my father when I was a small boy. Walking distance from the ocean, my frequent midnight strolls along Mission Beach went unnoticed by almost everyone. Positioned in a high traffic area for the local surfers, the shop could keep me much busier than I chose to be. At the present time, I hand-crafted one surfboard every few weeks, only for the people I really wanted to make them for, and never anyone who was in a rush.

"Mr. Eagan, you got anything today?"

I lowered my file, turned toward the door, and removed my dust mask. "Tell you what. I'll be done with this in about an hour, and then I'll get it gel-coated. Come back in say, three hours?"

"About four?" he asked.

Juan lived half a mile from the shop, and often did odd jobs for me. He was dressed in khakis, a white wife beater, and navy blue canvas slip-on sneakers, and he looked the part of every other gang-banger in the area, but he wasn't. He was a good kid. He was fourteen, Hispanic, and although I was fairly certain he was a US citizen, I suspected his father was an illegal immigrant. There were tens of thousands of illegals in the San Diego area, and many of the adults worked odd jobs for cash.

No one, however, was interested in hiring a teenager to do anything, illegal immigrant or not.

He started coming around my shop when he was ten. By the time he was twelve, his older brother was given a seven-year prison sentence for drug related crimes. Immediately following his brother's incarceration, he lashed out by spraying graffiti on many of the buildings along the boardwalk.

I decided hiring him to do odd jobs just might keep him from eventually traveling along the same path as his brother. Soon thereafter, I learned his work ethic was outstanding and everything he did was done with extreme caution and tremendous care. I had little doubt that whatever money he earned went straight to his family, probably assisting in their provisions for food or housing.

"That'll be fine, you can sweep the shop and take the trash to the bin," I said.

As I pulled my mask over my mouth, he turned toward the door. I watched him peer through the glass and into the street for some time, and after realizing he was in no hurry to leave, put down my file and walked toward him.

"Everything okay?" I asked.

He continued to stare out into the street. "You ever have something you didn't want to do, but part of you wanted to do it? Like the bad part of you?"

I chuckled. "The bad part, huh?"

He turned toward me and nodded. With his closely cut hair, tanned scalp, and lean muscular body, if he was a few years older he could pass for one of the many Marines in the city.

"I suppose so. I call it temptation. The fight within us between good and evil." I pointed to the bench beside my work bench. "Have a seat."

He sauntered over to the bench and sat. I walked to the small refrigerator I kept in the shop, grabbed an orange soda, and sat down beside him.

I handed him the bottle of soda. "Here."

"Thank you."

"Good and evil." I paused and wiped my hands on the thighs of my jeans. "Most of us have a line we've drawn in the sand. Good is on one side and evil is on the other."

He opened the soda on the edge of the bench, took a drink and nodded.

"Not everyone agrees on what is good or what is evil. We each have our own beliefs. But, no matter who we are or what we believe in, at some point in time, we're tempted to do what is evil," I said. "To cross the line we've personally drawn in the sand."

"Abuela says evil is black, good is white, and some people are colorblind," he said.

"Sounds like your abuela is a smart woman," I said.

"You know Big Lopez?" he asked.

I shook my head. "I don't think so."

He took another drink of soda and gazed down at the floor. "You remember my older brother, Luis?"

"Sure do."

"He worked for Big Lopez."

"And what? Has Big Lopez got the bad part of you arguing with the good?" I asked.

He finished the soda and nodded. "Big Lopez pays big money."

"And big money got your brother in prison for what, seven years?"

He nodded again. "Yep."

"You know, any time we consider doing something that's contrary to what we find acceptable, we naturally weigh the risk. It seems that's the deciding factor, each and every time. If the risk of getting caught is small, or if the punishment associated with the risk is small, we tell ourselves it's acceptable. If the risk is great, or if the punishment is great, we'll inevitably refuse. Selling drugs for Big Lopez seems like a pretty easy decision."

He shifted his eyes from the floor to the front of the shop and gazed outside. "But what if the guy offering the risk is mean, like Big Lopez?"

"He's mean, huh?" I asked.

He took the final drink of soda. "Yep."

"So, where's Big Lopez stay?" I asked.

"Barrio Logan. Or sometimes with his sister at Logan Heights," he said.

"By the Navy Base?"

"Yep."

"Well, what do *you* want to do?" I asked.

"You mean if I didn't have to worry about Big Lopez?"

"Yeah. If he wasn't a problem."

He glanced in my direction. "Keep doing what I'm doing. Luis says prison's no good. He said he's never going back."

"Well," I said as I stood. "Listen to your abuela, and don't become colorblind. And remember, things always have their own way of working out. Just give it a little more time. I'm sure everything will be fine."

He stood, turned to face me, and wiped the wrinkles from the legs of his khakis. "Mr. Eagan?"

I reached for the empty bottle. "Yeah?"

"I'll see you at four."

I tossed the bottle into the trash. "See you at four."

He walked to the door, pulled it open, and hesitated. As I pulled my mask over my mouth and grabbed the file, he peered over his shoulder. "Thank you."

I nodded and waved.

As I watched him ride away on his bicycle, I pulled off my mask, laid the file on the bench, and placed the surfboard in the rack. One more day wouldn't matter to the customer. One more day to Juan might change his life forever.

And I knew a little too much about altering the path of a child's life.

***

I walked into the restaurant, surveyed the few patrons, and fixed my eyes on who I suspected was Big Lopez.

Sitting alone at a table eating, he was wearing khakis, a plaid button-down, and had a hat on top of his very large head with the word BIG embroidered across the front. By my guess, he weighed an easy three hundred pounds.

Soft mariachi music filled the air as I walked directly to the table, pulled out the chair across from him, and sat down.

Without looking up from his plate of tamales, he spoke. His thick accent was a complete contrast to Juan's almost perfect English. "You lost?"

"You know," I said. "Temptation's a bitch."

He pushed his chair away from the table slightly and studied me. "Something you need to say?"

"Juan Ramirez, Luis' little brother. After Luis went to prison, I started looking after him. You know, like a big brother. And now I see my younger brother tempted to do something that I don't agree with."

I leaned forward, pressing my forearms into the edge of the table. "So, I've got to do what any big brother would do."

He wiped the corner of his mouth with his napkin and widened his eyes as if feigning interest.

"I've got to step in and make sure he does what's right," I said.

"That's what you're doing?" he asked with a deep laugh. "Stepping in?"

I leaned away from the table and nodded. "I've stepped in."

He pressed his thumb against the bill of his hat and lifted it slightly. "You think some guero throwing a buck-eighty at me is going to make me flinch?"

I glared back at him. "I look at Juan as my responsibility. He's not coming to work for you. Not now. Not ever. My best advice to you is to avoid him at all costs."

He glanced over each shoulder, fixed his eyes on mine, and grinned as he pulled his hat down tight against his head. "Hijo de la chingada. You got some balls, homie. Coming in here threatening me."

I shook my head. "I haven't threatened you. Yet."

Almost hidden by the bill of his hat, his brown eyes narrowed.

I stood from my seat glared at him. "Ask yourself this. Is the risk worth the reward?"

He tilted his head back slightly and gazed back at me. "Depends, Guero. What's my risk?"

Without responding, I turned and walked toward the door believing that some things were best left to the imagination.

And I had one hell of an imagination.

CHAPTER SEVEN

LIV

We walked along the beach no differently than we had a thousand times in the past, but to me, the experience was much more satisfying. I would have never guessed it to be possible, but I felt a deeper connection to Luke since we started having sex. I had convinced myself during my campaign to become fuck buddies that nothing between us would change, but things sure seemed to be different. The differences weren't things I could identify or pinpoint, but I had become much more satisfied in his presence than I had ever been before.

"How was Black's?" I asked, referring to his day of surfing at Black's Beach.

"Racetrack lefts all day, but the offshore wind kept 'em coming in, and I kept riding 'em," he said.

"Sounds like a good day."

"It was."

Lefts and rights were some of the types of waves, referencing whether or not the wave broke to the left or right. I understood very little of the terminology, but I knew enough to smile and nod if Luke was happy about his day of surfing.

"So," he said. "Are you enjoying this new arrangement?"

I was enjoying it, but didn't necessarily want him to fully understand just how much I was. At least not completely. I was afraid if he felt things were changing between us he would want to go back to the way things were. Personally, the thought of that *ever* happening was beginning to scare me.

"I am, are you?"

He nodded. "Strange, but I'm fucking loving it."

Strange?

"Why strange?" I asked.

"I just never thought we'd end up here," he said.

"Is that bad?" I asked.

"No," he said. "It's not bad, it's just seems odd. I mean, we've been friends for almost twenty years, and here we are. Friends with benefits."

I turned to him and grinned. "I like fuck buddies."

He chuckled. "Okay. Fuck buddies."

In the past, I often felt embarrassed when looking at Luke with his shirt off. Even at the beach, I felt a need to turn away after a quick glance, almost as if I didn't have the right to admire him. After we started fucking, I felt differently, and now enjoyed gawking at him at length.

As we walked along the edge of where the ocean met the sand, I pressed my toes into the beach and twisted them as we walked, trailing slightly behind Luke. He walked in a steady pace, and never really goofed off, always seeming to be on a mission with a much deeper meaning. After falling behind by a considerable amount, I would run to catch up, admiring the form of the muscles in his back all along the way.

"I don't want to sound like a weirdo," I said as I ran up to his side. "But you seem bigger than normal. You know, more muscular."

"Think so?" he asked.

"Uh huh," I said. "I do."

The San Diego sun was warm on my shoulders, but the breeze off the ocean was cool, as always. Luke seemed unaffected by the temperature changes, always wearing shorts and rarely wearing a shirt. He was a person who enjoyed nature much more than technology, and it seemed he felt a tighter connection to the earth the less clothing he wore.

"I may have gained a few pounds with all that you've been feeding me. That, and as much surfing as I've been doing. Carrying that board up and down to Black's is a bitch."

To the best of my knowledge, he didn't own a scale, and probably had no idea of what he even weighed. I, on the other hand, weighed myself sometimes more than once a day, always worried I was on my way to becoming obese, although I really knew it would never happen.

"Do you have a scale?" I asked.

"A what?"

"A scale."

"Like, to weigh myself?"

"Yeah."

"Sure don't. Can't see much sense in it."

I shrugged. "You'd know how much you weigh."

He stopped walking and turned to face me. "And what good would that do me?"

I stopped and twisted my hips back and forth, grinding my feet into the wet sand. "Well, you could see if you're gaining weight or losing it, and change your diet or whatever to try and be where you wanted to be. Just like everyone else who has one."

He glared at me for a second and turned away as if I had just recommended he rob a bank. After he was ten or fifteen feet away, I shook my head and ran to catch up.

"I was just wondering if you've gained weight, don't get all butt hurt." I chuckled.

He paused and turned toward me. "When I'm hungry, I eat. When I'm full I stop. I exercise because I enjoy it and it provides me peace of mind. A scale isn't going to change anything," he said.

"Fine. But you look like you've gained weight," I said.

"Good." He grinned. "I guess."

I liked how I could tell Luke he gained weight and he didn't care. Women, on the other hand, would be in tears after hearing the exact same thing.

"So, are you hungry?" I asked.

He glanced toward the sun. "Actually, I am."

Luke didn't own a watch. He was the type of person to gauge the time of day based on where the sun was in the sky. If the sun was rising, it was morning. If it was in mid-sky, it was noon, and when the sun set, it was night time. His life, in that one respect at least, was pretty simple.

I shielded my eyes with my palm, glanced toward the sun, and turned toward him as I lowered my hand. "Me too. Looks like it's about lunch time."

He glanced up the beach toward the boardwalk. "Smart ass."

Hand-in-hand we walked to *Draft*, a pub at the end of the boardwalk that faced the beach. We often held hands, something that started long before we began fucking. It was something I always admired about Luke. As masculine as he was, when it came to caring for those he loved, he knew no limits.

Luke's parents divorced when he was twelve, and it seemed he changed considerably immediately following his mother's departure from the family. I had the luxury of growing up with both parents, and as far-fetched as their separation was for me to imagine, it wasn't difficult for me to envision the difficulties Luke was faced with at the time.

In the first year following his mother's absence, not only did we become much closer as friends, but he and his younger brother became inseparable. It was then that we began holding hands in our walks to and from school, and I soon learned that Luke wasn't one to be bullied into – or out of – anything.

A group of kids at school gave him a hard time for holding hands with me, and called him a sissy. His hair at the time was long, not much different than most of the girls in school, but Luke was no sissy. One day on the way home from school, he proved it by fighting the entire group of boys.

After that, they avoided us on our walks home.

For the most part, we held hands ever since.

"So, I was thinking," I said.

"About?"

"Well, you said sex with you was going to be this big deal. Like it was going to turn me into a blubbering mess. I'm not complaining, but I've got to say so far I don't see what the big deal is."

"Do you remember me telling you I was going to take it slow and easy?"

"Uhhm. No, not really. We talked about a lot of stuff."

"Well, I did."

I bit the inside of my lip and gazed down at my menu, trying my best to think of the content of our many sexual conversations that followed my life altering Tinder date. I came up with nothing.

I shrugged. "I got nothing."

"Doesn't mean I didn't say it. Okay, here. I'll say it again," he said.

"Liv, I'm a sexual deviant. I don't think you're going to be able to keep up with my sexual needs when it comes right down to it, but we can give it a try. If we decide sex isn't working between us, we need to be sure we always remain friends. There, does that sound familiar?"

I shook my head. "Nope."

"You have a shit memory."

"You *think* things, and somehow you convince yourself when you think about it, we've talked about it. You've always been that way," I said.

He picked up his menu, opened it, and began to scan the pages for lunch options.

"Well, back to what I was saying. If you're wondering whether or not to turn up the heat, go right ahead. I'm good to go," I said.

He peered over the top of his menu and chuckled. "Good to go?"

"Yep. Good to go."

He shifted his eyes down to the menu. "We'll see about that."

"Sure will," I said.

Fucking Luke was good for me. Not only was it sexually satisfying, convenient, and fun, it convinced me I was more sexually diverse than I thought I was. Some of the things we were doing weren't things I ever would have done without him – and if asked by anyone, I probably would have declined. But with Luke, I felt no need to refuse, knowing I had nothing to lose if things went awry during one of our sexual romps.

I wasn't just becoming extremely content fucking him, I was slowly falling into a more comfortable place with him, one stroke at a time.

And it was scaring me.

"You want my suggestion?" he asked.

My face still artificially buried in my menu, I responded in a carefree tone hinting at a lack of interest. "Sure."

"Eat a light lunch," he said.

"Oh really?"

"Yeah." He folded his menu closed. "I don't want you to barf later when we're going at it."

"I'll be fine," I said.

He brushed his hair away from his face and grinned. "Yeah, you're *good to go.*"

I lowered my menu and glared at him. "What makes you think I'm not?"

"You may be, I don't know. I haven't got much experience to go on, but based on what I do know, we'll reach a point where you give up."

"What makes you so sure?"

He shrugged. "I'm a weirdo."

"I don't think so. So far, I've loved everything."

He grinned a playful grin. "On a scale of one to ten, I've probably given you a three. My mind goes in weird places."

"So, what is it that gets you off?"

He shrugged again and shifted his focus to the restaurant's open wall that faced the beach. "I don't know. Weird stuff. Thinking that you're confused. Or suffering. Not suffering like you'd think, but mentally suffering. I don't know, it's hard to explain."

"What do you want to do to me? Can you tell me?"

"You know Valerie and I broke up over sex. She said I was too unpredictable. She said I liked knowing she was willing more than I actually liked her."

"Well, we both know that's not the case here," I said.

"I know," he said. "But that doesn't mean you'll agree to everything.

Or that I won't make you take a step back and say *what the fuck were you thinking?* That day's gonna come, I'm sure of it. Fuck, I don't know. Just know that whatever happens, I don't want to do anything to make you uncomfortable, so if that day or that time comes, you let me know. I guess being friends with benefits has its perks, because when I do something stupid, we can sit back and talk about it, right?"

"Right," I said.

"So, hell, it doesn't even matter. If you decide I'm some weirdo, we'll just quit, right?"

I tried to convince myself he was right, but regardless of how I looked at it, it *did* matter. As convinced as he was that he was a sexual deviant, I sure didn't see it. I couldn't help but wonder if his one and only love, Valerie, was just a prude.

She went to school with us, and as much as I hated her, Luke chose to date her through the end of school and until he was twenty years old. As hard as I tried, I could never imagine them lasting, and was actually quite relieved when they broke up. Personally, I thought she was a self-important bitch.

"So what if it isn't you? What if you're just adventurous, and Valerie was some prude?"

He shook his head. "I don't think so."

I shrugged. "Might be true."

"Doubtful," he said.

"What would be like, I don't know, your perfect sexual experience?"

He gazed beyond me for a moment and stared out at the beach. After a short time, he shifted his gaze to meet mine. "All kinds of things, especially something that confuses you or mixes you up. Like fucking you while you were trying to compose a really important email at your office. Or while you were on a deadline at work with a few minutes to spare. Or maybe while you were in a conference giving a speech or something."

I squinted. "Fucking me while I'm in a meeting?"

"Yeah."

"Wow. Yeah, that's kind of weird. I mean, not like bad weird, but like *weird*, weird. Huh, that's interesting."

As we sat silently for a moment, I thought about what his sexual fantasies were. They all seemed to be with causing me to lose my focus on something critical or important.

"Why do you think you're the way you are? You know, sexually?" I asked.

"It's hard to say," he said, his eyes falling to the floor. "I'm sure there's a reason for it, though."

For some reason, I felt like he knew why, but was embarrassed to say. I just had a feeling. Call it women's intuition. Maybe it was because we were best friends for our entire life, and I knew him so well. Whatever the reason, I wasn't convinced he was being completely truthful.

Regardless, I felt better about my being able to keep up with his sexual demands. His interest seemed to be fucking me into a state of confusion, and that would be a pretty simple task as far as I was concerned.

"Okay," I said as I tossed the menu aside. "A light lunch it is. And when we get home, you can fuck me until I lose clarity."

"Doubt that would take much," he said dryly.

I flipped him my middle finger and grinned. "And I'll think a little bit about the at work thing. Maybe, and I mean maybe, we'll be able to do something with that."

FUCK BUDDY

He shook his head as he waved toward the waitress. "In the meantime, I'm sure I'll think of something."

I was sure he would, and I hoped whatever he thought of included time for us to snuggle when we were done.

Although my sexual appetite was being fed, I felt my recovery from the sex was lacking. As caring as Luke was, I guessed if I mentioned it the next time we had sex, he'd agree. Hell, maybe he had a fetish for it and I just didn't know about it.

Yet.

I glanced across the table as the waitress walked up. As he pointed to the menu, she eyed him like she wanted to eat him.

Sorry, bitch, he's mine.

Well, kind of.

CHAPTER EIGHT

LUKE

"Everything?"

"Whatever your perception of naked is," I responded.

"Sounds like everything." Liv responded softly, her gaze falling to my waist.

Over the years, I had seen Liv in a swimsuit, wearing skimpy outfits, and wrapped in a towel after a shower. I had never, however, seen her naked until we started our new arrangement. Her body was about as perfect as I would imagine anyone's could be, and seeing her undress was a gift in itself. I stood at the end of her bed and watched as she undressed, treasuring the removal of each article of clothing.

Liv wasn't a tall woman, but I wouldn't describe her as short, either. Standing five foot four, I liked to call her average height. She was graced with a nice round ass, reasonably large breasts, and a defined waist between them.

Clothed, she looked tempting. Naked, she looked irresistible.

"Okay," she said as she tossed her panties into the pile.

She stood, nervously twisting her hips back and forth, and forced a grin. I raised my hand to my chin and studied her.

"What?"

I folded my arms in front of my chest. "Nothing, just admiring you."

"Is there something wrong?"

"No, nothing at all. In fact," I said as I slowly walked around her. "You look perfect."

"Whatever. I'm a little fatty," she said.

"I think you're perfect."

"Are you going to get undressed?" she asked over her shoulder.

Standing behind her, I placed my hands against each side of her waist. I raised them slowly, enjoying every inch of her smooth skin until the tips of my fingers rested at the edge of her breasts. "I may."

"Oh," she cooed.

I turned to face her and admired her perfectly sculpted breasts. Her eyes followed my hand I reached toward her with an extended finger. With the tip, I gently traced around the circumference of her nipple repeatedly.

She inhaled a quick breath.

"So, I was thinking," I said as I stepped in front of her. "I'm going to have you read a book while I fuck you. Like, out loud."

"Huh? Read a book?" she snapped back.

"Yeah."

"I think…" She swallowed, exhaled, and licked her lips. "I think I want you to choke me."

I cocked my head to the side and met her gaze. "Choke you? While you read a book?"

She swallowed again and shook her head lightly. "I don't care. If the book makes you happy, sure. I really want you to choke me. My twat is dripping down my leg from thinking about it. Maybe we can do it after the reading part?"

The thought of choking her excited me, but it was something I perceived as taboo, especially with someone I cherished as much as Liv. I often fantasized about such things, but viewed them as off-limits, and therefore never considered introducing them into my sexual activities. Liv had always been special to me, and since our new arrangement began to unfold, she had become even more so.

I had limited myself to strange sexual situations to satisfy my kink, and to be honest, had been mentally searching for something new and exciting for us to consider. If me choking her was something she felt she would enjoy, I wondered what else may arouse her.

As much as I wanted to refuse her request, I decided if it was something she truly wanted, and something I yearned to do, maybe I would proceed with caution.

I cocked an eyebrow. "You really want me to choke you?"

She nodded repeatedly. "Uh huh."

"While I'm fucking you?"

"It'd be kinda weird if you did it while I was eating dinner," she said with a laugh. "Yeah, while you're fucking me."

I laughed at her response. Excited at the thought of choking her, but slightly uncomfortable with the implementation, I stood silently for a moment and gazed blankly at her.

"When you choked me the other day for just a second, I really liked it. Since we talked at the bar, I've been thinking. If you want to confuse me while you're fucking me, choking me is a good way to do it, so maybe it'd be a turn-on for both of us."

It wasn't at all what I expected to hear. "You liked it when I grabbed you neck?"

"Uh huh. And when I think about it, my pussy turns into a river."

My cock stiffened as she spoke. "Alright then, we'll do both."

"Both?"

"Yeah, while you're trying to read, I'll choke you *and* fuck you."

"You know; this is just fucking weird. I'm standing here naked talking about this shit and you're standing there looking like you're going to the beach. We need to just do this shit. I mean, I'm up for pretty much anything. Just, I don't know, do whatever you want. Spontaneity would be nice. But *this*." She waved her hand back and forth between us. "This whole negotiation thing ruins the mood."

I couldn't agree with her more. I grabbed her Kindle from the night stand beside her bed. After thumbing through the available books, I opened one and flipped to a random page.

I handed her the device. "I agree. But, no differently than handing a man a rifle doesn't make him a trained soldier, a man having a willing participant doesn't make him a BDSM Master or Dom or whatever. This is all new to me. We'll get through it."

She grinned. "Okay."

She glanced at the Kindle and then shifted her eyes to meet mine. "So, what now?"

"Climb on the bed, lay down, and start reading."

"Belly or back?" he asked.

"Back."

As she climbed onto the bed, I pulled off my shorts and tossed my shirt beside the bed. Her earlier complaint was certainly a valid one, as my previously rigid cock was now almost flaccid and seemed to lack interest in even continuing.

"Start where you have it opened?" she asked.

My level of arousal had dropped completely. The mere mention of choking her had taken my mind in a different direction altogether. In an effort to convince myself I didn't *need* to choke her, I responded.

"Sure. Wherever," I said.

Laying on her back gazing up at the Kindle, she cleared her throat and began. *"Although she hadn't seen Trayvor in thirteen years, nothing had changed, she thought."*

"Do you want me to keep going?"

On my knees at the foot of the bed, I glanced down at my cock. "Sure, keep going."

"Nervously, she cleared her throat. She had hoped to explain her dilemma without much emotion, but doing so in his presence quickly became seemingly impossible. She studied him as he inched closer, her eyes fixed on his hands."

"More?" she asked.

The most beautiful woman I had ever seen was laying before me, and she wanted me to fuck her. My mind – and my cock – apparently had zero interest. I wanted to choke her, and as I gazed down at her naked body, I realized there was really nothing that was going to act as a viable substitute.

"Just a little more," I said.

"Her fascination with his hands began early in their relationship. He had once…"

I gazed down at her naked body. With her face obstructed by the Kindle she held in her hands, I cautiously crawled between her legs as she continued to read.

"A slight shimmer from the chrome barrel caught her attention. Naturally, she took a step back with her…"

I slapped the Kindle out of her hands and to the far side of her bed. Startled, she stared back at me, her face washed with concern. Without warning, I reached down, gripped her neck in my hands, and began to squeeze.

Her eyes widened and she groaned out one dry word.

"Harder…"

She had said all I needed to hear. I tightened my grip on her neck as I pushed my hips between her thighs. My level of arousal was at an all-time high. Starving for the feeling of her tight pussy's clench on my throbbing shaft, I forced myself into her. It was as if a completely different cock was between my legs.

I began to thrust my hips savagely, shouting as I did so.

"Focus, Liv. Focus!" I bellowed as I pounded myself deeper and deeper.

She arched her back.

I tightened my grip and shoved my entire weight against her, hoping to force every last inch of myself into her.

"God damn it, Liv. You've got to focus. You'll never amount to anything if you can't focus," I screamed.

I released my grip with my right hand and pressed the web of my left hand against her neck, pushing her down into the comforter of the bed. Her eyes followed my right hand as I raised it high above her.

Whack!

I slapped her face and screamed. "For fuck's sake, Luke. Focus."

I felt her pussy tighten against my shaft as I ground my hips between her thighs. I raised my hand again. Her lips parted slightly. I shifted my gaze to her bouncing breasts. I swept my hand down toward her chest, slapping the tips of my fingers harshly against her tit.

My breathing quickly became labored. I felt my scrotum tighten. I released her neck, gripped her butt with each hand, and lifted her from the bed. The tips of my fingers dug deep into the flesh of her ass as I shoved every inch of myself deep into her soaking wet mound. I held my hips against her inner thighs and closed my eyes. Soon, my back arched and I groaned loudly, feeling a level or satisfaction that was totally new to me. At the same time, Liv wailed into the room.

"Oh…fuuuuuck," she cried.

Magically, our bodies, minds, and spirits seemed to connect. Her pussy clenched against the shaft of my cock, all but begging me to reach climax. In response, it swelled in size, receptive to her inner desires.

Together, we each moaned into the room, reaching climax at precisely the same time.

My vision blurred as the cum rushed from me. A few short unsuspecting strokes later, and I held myself deep within her, cherishing the feeling of our bodies being bound together.

I collapsed onto the bed beside her.

"Holy. Shit." She turned her head to face me. "That. Was fucking. Crazy."

I met her gaze and grinned. "So, you enjoyed it?"

She pressed her elbow into the bed and rested her cheek against the palm of her hand. "Fuck..."

The tone of her voice led me to believe she was extremely pleased. She inhaled a shallow breath and bit into her quivering lip. As she exhaled, she murmured the remaining portion of her response. "I. Loved it."

"Me too. Sorry about the slapping. I don't know what happened."

"Sorry, Not sorry." She chuckled. "It was so fucking hot. Holy crap."

"Yeah," I breathed. "It was."

We relaxed side by side, catching our breath and regaining our composure. After a few moments of silence, she tossed her legs over the edge of the bed and stood.

"I'm gonna pee," she said.

"Okay."

Her long brown hair hung to the middle of her narrow back. Now a complete mess, watching her walk to the bathroom with it unkempt was satisfying in itself. A few minutes later she returned, her hair still knotted, grinning as she climbed into the bed.

"Holy crap. I was *full* of cum. Like full. It leaked out *forever*. Excited much?"

"I got pretty excited." I chuckled.

She nestled beside me and stared up at the ceiling. "I've got a question."

"Okay."

"Uhhm. When you were slapping me, you said 'Focus Luke.' You said *your* name. What was that about?"

"I said 'Liv', not 'Luke.' "

"I think you said 'Luke.' 'For fuck's sake, Luke. Focus.' "

I shook my head. "I think you were confused."

She turned her head to the side. "Well, I guess that's what you were after. To fuck me until I was confused, right?"

"I suppose so," I said with a laugh. "Now, roll over here and put your head on my shoulder. I want to just lay here and hold you."

She grinned. "Okay."

After she positioned herself against me, we talked of life, failed relationships, and our love for all things we found to be beautiful. As the night progressed, the length of time between subjects increased, and eventually – without much warning – we fell asleep.

Each of us at basically the same time.

For the first time since I was a child, I slept all night without dreams, without waking, and without the desire to walk down to the beach for comfort.

My comfort, it seemed, was at my side.

CHAPTER NINE

LIV

"If you say a word, I'll kill you," I said.

She shook her head. "I won't, I swear."

"Dead. Like to the cemetery. That kind of dead," I said in my most convincing tone.

She pulled away front he table slightly and squinted. "Okay. Jeez. I said I won't."

"Luke."

She scrunched her nose. "Huh?"

I nodded and grinned. "Luke."

"Luke? Like Luke fucking Eagan? The surfer? Your bestie?" she screeched.

I glanced over each shoulder. "Shhh."

Chloe and I were sitting in a restaurant eating lunch. With her arms covered in colorful Asian themed tattoos and rocking a black and purple ombré, she didn't look much differently than she did the last time I had seen her. Well, with the exception of the hair color, but her hair was always colored wildly.

"Holy shit, Liv. Are you serious?"

"Uh huh."

"For how long?"

FUCK BUDDY

I shrugged. "I dunno. Like a couple of months. No, maybe a little more than a month."

She widened her eyes, swallowed heavily, and stared in apparent disbelief. "One word. *Wow*."

My face washed with pride. "Uh huh."

"God, I remember when we were in school. No disrespect, but I wanted that guy to fuck me so bad. He was so fucking hot," she said, shaking her head lightly. "Then, I saw him on T.V a while back. They did a thing on him on News 8 like a year ago, did you see that?"

"No, but I heard about it."

"It was freaking nuts. He was inside some crazy thirty-footer at Black's. The swell kept swallowing him up, and he's inside the barrel just riding it like it's no big deal. Over and over, he'd just disappear into the tube or whatever, and then *bam*, out he'd come," she said, holding her arms out to the side, giving her best surfer imitation.

She glanced down at the table and quickly raised her eyes to meet mine. "It was when we had that big storm like early last spring. The whole beach was there watching him. Nobody would even try and paddle out. But Luke? Yeah, he was out there, just like always."

Chloe was a slut, but she was a funny slut. Although I hadn't seen her in eighteen months, I really felt like there was no one else I could talk to about Luke without being chastised or criticized. She had always been a little bit of a weirdo when it came to sex, and seemed to always have boyfriends who like to slap her around.

Since our odd phone sex encounter, I decided to give her another call and see if she had time to meet for lunch and talk.

She shook her head. "Anyway, holy fuck. So, does he fuck as good as he surfs?"

"Uhhm. Yeah, probably better. But I've got some questions."

"About what?"

"Well, about wild sex. He's into all kinds of weird stuff."

"No shit. Like having you call me on the phone while you're boning. That was funny. Kavin's a freak, too. So what's the question?" she asked.

I twisted in my seat nervously. "Uhhm. Well, have any of your boyfriends liked to choke you?"

"Uh, yeah. Like all of 'em."

"Oh." I giggled. "Sorry."

She twirled the ends of her hair around her index finger and snapped her gum repeatedly. "So Luke's a freak, huh?"

I quickly remembered what it was I didn't like about her. The gum thing drove me insane from the first time we met. Apparently she didn't grow out of it.

I shrugged and took a sip of my malt. "I guess so. So, I'm guessing you like that kinky stuff?"

"Kinky? Yeah, love it. But choking isn't kinky, it's just whatever. I mean, really, Anastasia Steele's got nothing on me."

I wrinkled my nose. "Who?"

"Seriously?" She chuckled. "Fifty Shades of Grey? Anastasia? Christian? Hello?"

"Oh, yeah. I didn't see it," I said.

"Did you read the book?"

I shook my head. "Nope."

"Do you like Luke's hand on your neck?"

I stared blankly.

"When he chokes you, do you like it?"

"Oh. Yeah, I do."

"Read the book. It's a joke as far as BDSM goes, but it's a good read. Might make you realize some things about yourself."

"Okay." I took another sip of my malt. "You said choking wasn't kinky. So, what's kinky?"

She stopped twirling her hair. "You poor thing. You haven't got a clue, do you?"

I shook my head.

"I'll give you a few of my faves. Bondage, spankings, deprivation, piss play, butt plugs, and a good face fucking. I mean, really, there's not much I don't like," she said.

A lump rose in my throat. I swallowed twice, gazed at her wide-eyed, and coughed. "Piss play? You don't…"

"Sure do. He pissed all over me, and I love it. Hey, it's not for everyone, but don't knock it. So, are you submissive?"

I shrugged. The thought of being pissed on, even by Luke, made me cringe. I gazed back at her, filled with wonder.

"But Luke's dominant, right?"

I shrugged again. It seemed like a rhetorical question. All men were dominant as far as I knew.

"Oh shit. Please, tell me you've got a safe word at least."

"A what?"

Her mouth fell agape. "Liv! You two idiots are going to fuck around and hurt someone. Oh my god. Do you have a laptop?"

"Yeah."

She began twisting her hair in her finger again. "Just Google BDSM and start reading all you can. Jesus. Have Luke do the same. Jesus fuck. Google what a safe word is. It's a word you two agree on, and when you've had enough, or you're uncomfortable, you say it, and whatever is going on, no matter what, stops. It's to keep you safe and him out of jail."

I leaned forward and cleared my throat. "Don't get mad, but what does BDSM stand for. I mean, I kind of know, but I don't."

She rolled her eyes as she shook her head. "You're funny. So, you kind of know and you kind of don't, huh? It's okay. BDSM stands for a lot of things. The B and D stand for bondage and discipline. Then, the D and S stand for dominance and submission. And, the S and the M stand for sadism and masochism."

"Oh, yeah. Luke said he read about himself and he's a maso-whatever."

"He's a masochist?"

I nodded. "That's what he said."

She grinned. "Nice. Hope you like being humiliated and you're into pain."

"It's okay. I mean I like so far. But, can I ask you more?"

She glanced at her watch. "I've got to go in about thirty, but sure."

"We were having sex and he slapped me. Like hard. Really hard. And he choked me really hard. And. Well. I uhhm, I liked it. I mean I *really* liked it. So, is there something wrong with me? I mean, I wasn't like abused or anything when I was a kid."

She laughed a gentle laugh. "No, there's nothing wrong with you. There's hundreds of thousands of people just like you and me. Here's the math."

She glanced over each shoulder and craned her neck as she peered past me and around the restaurant. "Well, seven out of ten fantasize about it, and four out of ten are into it. In this restaurant right now, there's twenty people. So, there's two more in here just like us. And these types of relationships are healthy, as long *as you have a safe word.*"

"Wow, really? So you know a lot about this Where do you get all your, you know, information?"

She shrugged. "Reading. Munches..."

"What's a munch?"

"A meeting with other people who are into it. It's just a gathering. Like when the surfers gather around a bonfire. Only it's Doms and subs at a hotel banquet room or whatever."

"Really?"

"Yea, really."

"Wow. Okay," I said. "I really appreciate all the help."

"Luke." She shook her head and grinned. "Who would have guessed you'd bag Luke fucking Eagan. Wow. You know, I thought you'd just be besties forever."

"I know, right?"

I wasn't really embarrassed about it, but I decided not to tell her we were just fuck buddies.

"Okay, I need to get. So, what's the first thing you're going to do?"

"Uhhm. Safe word."

She slid out of the booth and stood. "Give me a call anytime. I mean it."

I gave her a hug and told her goodbye. After a moment of contemplation, I sat down in the booth and decided to stay for a few more minutes. I checked my phone for text messages, and upon seeing I had none, opened my browser and typed "safe word" into Google.

I read what popped up on the phone's screen and scrolled down to the images. After clicking on a pair of handcuffs and opening all of the Google photos associated with the search, I began to click through the images.

Five minutes later, and I was anxious and horny.

Ten minutes after that, and I typed "how do I know if I'm submissive" into Google. A few minutes and one test later, and the results popped up:

Hello, subbie. You're 88% submissive.

I stared at the screen and grinned.

I think it's time Luke and I had another talk.

CHAPTER TEN

LUKE

I stood at the door of the paint booth and admired the contrast between white and orange. I may have been colorblind, but I wasn't blind to beauty. The board was beautiful.

The door opening diverted my attention from the board to the other side of the shop.

"You Luke?" the man asked.

"Sure am. How can I help you?"

He appeared to be in his early thirties, had shoulder-length sun-bleached hair that resembled a cotton ball, and the skin tone of a man who spent his leisure time in the sun. Dressed in seasonal attire of shorts and a surf tank, he looked at home in the shop.

"I need a board built," he said.

"If you're in a hurry, you'll need to go somewhere else."

He glanced around the shop. "Waited this long, so a little longer won't hurt."

"You a local?"

"El Cajon."

"Where's your favorite spot?"

I found that asking people how well they surfed – or to describe their abilities – left far too much up to interpretation. A surfer's pride in himself often caused responses to be slightly more braggadocio and far less accurate. The location of their favorite spot told me much more information about what types of waves they were able to ride, and how fast or slow the board needed to be.

"Right here," he said, tossing his head toward the door.

"Good old Mission Beach. Ever hit Oceanside Pier, Scripp's, Cardiff, or Black's?"

"I could hit those spots, but I don't. Well, all but Black's." He coughed a laugh. "I'm too young to die. Especially doing something I enjoy as much as surfing."

His responses provided all the information I needed to hear to agree to make him a board. As always, however, I was curious.

"Why here?"

"Dude. Really? You're Luke Eagan. I spent a lot of time wondering why you were so much better than everyone else, and after a few years of watching you at Black's and up at Seal, it just came to me. You know, no disrespect, but everyone says you're an arrogant prick."

I placed my hands on my hips and grinned.

He ran his hands through his blonde fluff and continued. "When I surf, I try to get in a zone, you know, clear my head of everything else. Doesn't really work, but it sounds good. But when I watched you for all that time, I realized something. For you, there *is* nothing else. Ever. You're not a prick, you're just focused."

Many people watched me surf, but I had always been humbled by those who watched me out of desire and not out of interest.

"I appreciate it," I said.

He brushed the sand from his shorts, and then looked like he was embarrassed for having done so. He glanced up and grinned. "When a man makes something with his hands, a small part of him is transferred to what it is he's crafted. At least that's my belief. Not too many making boards by hand anymore."

Completely satisfied by his response, I stood silently and let it resonate within me.

"So, that's why I'm here," he said.

"Why do you surf?" I asked.

He narrowed his eyes. "Why?"

"Yeah, why."

"Kind of hard for me to explain," he said.

"Give it a try."

He gazed down at the floor. After a moment, he shifted his eyes up to meet mine. "I don't know that everyone would agree with me, but I think I'm part of this earth. You know, nature. I mean, I'm not some man-made piece of machinery. For me to embrace life, I need to embrace nature. Become one with the earth. There's two ways to do that as far as I'm concerned. Floating through the sky or surfing. I'm afraid of heights. So, I surf. Or I try at least."

I cleared my throat. "You like short, mushy waves?"

He nodded.

"I can make you a fishy little board that'll be easy to ride, and give you a lot of speed if you want it. I can make the rocker flat enough to go fast, and have enough curve to get the turns you want. Something with a low entry, a little bit low through the center, and then the tail will need to drop out," I said.

"What are you? About five nine?" I asked.

"Exactly," he said.

"I'd recommend about four inches shorter than you are tall. About five-five. Single concave in the center, and into a double at the fins. It'll be an easy board – but have a lot of maneuverability – and it'll be fast on low waves. Everybody wants to go fast."

"How much time are you thinking?" he asked.

I shrugged. "How's two weeks from Friday sound?"

"Sounds awesome. Depending on what time you get it done, I might get some surfing in. I'm off on Fridays. We're working four tens right now. By the way, I'm Perry," he said as he extended his hand.

I shook his hand and grinned. "Luke. And I'll have it done late on the Thursday night before. So, you can pick it up Friday anytime."

He reached for his wallet. "Pay for it now?"

"Pay when you take it out of the shop. After you're sure you want it, I said. "Six hundred sound good?"

"Sounds cheap for a Luke Eagan custom."

"Tell you what," I said. "After you pick it up, we'll go down to the beach and I'll give you some tips."

He folded his arms in front of his chest and leaned back as if waiting for the punch line to a joke. "You're not serious. Are you?"

I clenched my fist, extended my thumb and pinkie finger, and twisted it back and forth. In Hawaii the gesture was called the *shaka*, in California, we surfers called the *hang loose* or *hang ten*. In any culture it was a greeting, a departure and a smile – all in one.

"My girl works till 3:30, so whatever time you get here, we'll just head down there," I said.

"Dude. Wow. Yeah. I'll uhhm. I'll be here at like. Yeah, what time do you open?"

I chuckled. "I live upstairs. I open when the sun comes up."

He ran his fingers through his hair and grinned. "Right on."

"Okay. See you two weeks from Friday," I said. "And it was nice to meet you, Perry."

He reached toward me with his open hand. "Yeah, same."

I shook his hand and he walked away, gazing around the shop as he left. All of the surf shops I had ever been in sold boards, leashes, shoes, shirts, trinkets, necklaces, sunglasses, and everything else a person may want for a day at the beach.

Other than the desire, my shop sold everything needed to surf.

Surfboards and fins. And that was it.

The walls were lined with surfboards, none of which were for sale. Each one held with it a memory. A place in time, an accomplishment, an unavoidable situation, or a turning point.

I glanced at the most recent addition to my collection.

Placed on the wall on the day Liv and I had sex for the first time, the board was one of my personal favorites. A long high-performance step-up with a single concave throughout, it was the board I began riding the day after the previous year's big storm. I glanced beside it. A high performance short that was flat at the feet and had a slight "V" at the tail was one I had ridden from the time Valerie and I broke up until the day of the storm. Some of the best waves I had caught were on that particular board, and the memories held with it were rich.

I grinned as I turned and admired teach of the boards. The memories they brought with them was better than a photograph or an embellished story that changed as it was told over time.

My life, one board at a time, was on display for all to see.

But, no differently than when a person watched me surf, the observer had no idea what was beyond the surface of what they were seeing.

None at all.

CHAPTER ELEVEN

LIV

The ocean provided me a level of peace that made it impossible to think about living anywhere that didn't have access to a beach. After high school, my parents moved to St. Louis. I chose to stay in San Diego and go to college. My father's job required them to move; but to me, San Diego was my home. By the time I was five I had lived in Chicago and Washington, D.C., but southern California was the only place I really remembered.

With my heels pressed against my butt and my knees tight to my chest, I gazed out at the horizon. As far as I could see, there was nothing but water. Gentle waves washed up to the shore, bringing with them the bits and pieces of life too weak to resist the strength of the current.

"If I was going to compare you to something out there," I said, tossing my head toward the horizon. "It'd be a shark."

Luke raised his head from the towel and turned to the side. "A shark?"

"Uh huh."

"Sharks are assholes. I'm not a shark. They're predators. I'd say I'd have to be…" he paused and lowered his head.

"A starfish," he said as he glanced up. "They can recover from their wounds – even vicious ones. They can regenerate even if they're cut in two, and some species can grow an entire new starfish from the severed leg of another."

"I wanna be a starfish," I said.

"You can be a clownfish. They're beautiful and playful. Hell, everyone loves a clownfish."

"I hate clowns," I said. "And I don't want to be a fish that looks like one. We can both be starfish."

He chuckled. "Okay. And remind me when Halloween comes. I need to dress up like a clown."

"Last year you were a pimp," I said. "With a purple fur coat."

"And you were my hooker."

"That was a good party," I said.

The previous Halloween, my boss invited me to his costume party. He lived in an upscale neighborhood in La Jolla, and had invited most of the people from the office to attend. Luke and I went together, which wasn't uncommon, but the party was. Amongst some of the city's richest residents, we had an absolute blast, playing the part of the hooker and the pimp.

Neither of us were as drunk as everyone else at the party. Partially because our sober state, but more so due to Luke's fabulous dance moves, we won late-night dance contest. All in all, the party was a great time, and the memories of it were still fresh on my mind.

It seemed I pushed some memories out of my mind completely to make room for the precious ones I wanted to keep. The Halloween party was a keeper.

"No," he said. "It was a great party. Good times. Really good times."

He rolled onto his back and brushed the sand from his chest and stomach. His mid-summer tan was deep and dark, and the top layer of his hair had become a light brown. Each time he swiped his hand across his stomach, the muscles on his upper arm flared. At times, for me at least, it was easy to get lost in admiring Luke.

This was one of those times.

Resting on his elbows with his shoulders elevated from the towel, he gazed out at the ocean. "Beautiful, isn't it?"

"I was just thinking the same thing," I responded.

I turned to face him. "Could you live without surfing?"

He continued to silently stare for some time before responding. "I suppose so. I wouldn't like it, but I could."

"Without the ocean?"

"Wow. I don't like thinking about it, but yeah. I could."

"The two things you love the most," I said. "And you could do without 'em. Not me. I can't imagine not having the ocean. That's what I've been thinking about."

"If you grew up in fucking Denver or whatever – no, let's say Omaha. If you grew up in fucking Omaha, Nebraska or something. Yeah, let's say Omaha, and your parents moved to St. Louis after high school. Would you have gone?" he asked.

"Are you in Omaha with me?"

He shook his head and laughed. "No, Liv. I'm right here. Kicking it at the beach in SD."

"Probably," I responded. "There wouldn't have been any reason for me to stay."

"So did you stay here for the beach or for me?" he asked.

I gazed out across the endless ocean. "A little of both."

He continued to sit and silently stare toward the horizon. After a moment, I cleared my throat and began a new line of questioning. "What are you not willing to give up? You said you could lose surfing and the ocean and live through it. But what would crush you?"

"What would crush me if I lost it? That's an easy one," he responded.

He tilted his head toward me. "You. I can't imagine not having you. Cant, and wont."

My throat constricted and my mouth went dry. I swallowed hard and grinned. "That's sweet. Thank you."

"It's true. No need to thank me." He rolled from the towel, pushed himself up to his knees, and stood.

I tried to hide my excitement from hearing him say he couldn't live without me, but I doubt I did a good job. I'd never been good at hiding much of anything, and my feelings were no exception.

He loomed over me, seeming much taller than he actually was. "What are you thinking about?"

I scrunched my nose and acted like I was searching for an answer, but I didn't have to. I was thinking of him. Being with him on a bigger scale. For real. In a relationship. A real relationship.

"You," I said.

There, I said it.

"What about me?"

"Everything."

He laughed. "You're thinking about everything about me?"

"Don't be difficult. No, not *everything*. Just, I don't know. Thinking."

"That's what I'm asking, Liv. About what? You've been staring out at the waves for the last hour and a half. What's on your mind?"

I knew better than to tell him the truth. We'd talked about it too many times, and he made himself crystal clear. Luke was scared to death of losing me, and even though I knew there was nothing he could do to cause me to leave him, convincing him of that was impossible. He felt whatever caused his relationship with Valerie to end was something that naturally occurred as a result of him being who he was.

Although I didn't know exactly what it was that caused the breakup, I also knew it didn't matter, at least not for now. I actually had everything I needed with our current arrangement. I had Luke, I spent as much time with him as I would if we were married, and we were having sex.

"I was just thinking how grateful I am to have you in my life," I said.

I stretched my legs out, quickly realizing Luke was right. I had been sitting in the same spot with my calves scrunched into the backs of my thighs for longer than I had thought. I wrinkled my nose and squinted as I rubbed my thighs with my hands.

"And I'm grateful to have you in mine. Are you alright?"

"I think I sat there for too long. My legs are killing me," I said as I tried to stand.

"Here," he said a she shook the sand from the towel. "Lay down. I'll rub them."

As he knelt down between my feet and rubbed my legs free of cramps, I watched the sun slowly melt into the ocean. As the sky turned to the most beautiful shades of oranges, deep blues and pinks, I realized Luke could see the same colors I saw, and it saddened me.

"What color do you see when you look at the sunset?"

He stopped rubbing my legs. "Orange and blue."

"No pink?" I asked.

"I don't see any," he said.

"So you still see most of the colors in the sunset, just not all of them?"

"I don't see them the same as you see them. But I see them," he said.

"Is it beautiful?" I asked.

"It sure is," he said.

His hand softly gripped my shoulder and he carefully turned me from my stomach onto my back. He brushed his hair from his eyes and held his hand in place to keep it from falling down again. As our eyes met, he grinned. "And so are you."

He leaned into me and kissed me fully, removing the memory of the sunset and replacing it with a new one. One of him kissing me on the beach as the sun set in front of us.

As he kissed me, I realized I *was* in a relationship with him. It just wasn't something a person could put a conventional label on.

And, for the time being, I wanted nothing to change.

CHAPTER TWELVE

LUKE

She opened the door and stepped aside. "Come in, Sir. I didn't want to ruin it at the beach, so I didn't say anything. Well, that and I wanted to do some more research first."

"Sir? Where the hell did that come from? Research? And what the fuck is that around your neck?"

She was wearing jeans, black heels, and a tight-fitting black button-down top. None of her clothing seemed too out of place – at least not for her. The wide black leather studded strap around her neck, however, did.

She motioned toward the living room. "I'll be in the living room, Sir."

I stepped past her and walked into the kitchen, my eyes remaining locked on her ridiculous leather necklace until I was half way to the refrigerator. "I need a yogurt. And what the fuck with the *sir* shit?"

I searched through the flavors of yogurt, looking for coconut. After determining there was none, I grabbed a cherry and shut the refrigerator door. "And why's your hair up like that?"

"It's called a tendril. It's sexy. I did it for you," she responded from the other room.

I grabbed a spoon and walked into the living room. As I entered, she was pacing back and forth across the living room floor. I stopped, pressed my hands against my hips, and shook my head. "What in the hell is going on?"

Some women looked like fools as they attempted to walk in heels. Others looked sophisticated, placing one foot directly in front of the other, their posture and their gait elegant as they took each well-placed step.

Liv was the latter.

She continued as I sat down. I peeled the foil top off of the yogurt, licked it, and shoved the spoon into the container.

Slowly, she paced the length of the room, gazing down at the floor as she walked past.

I lifted the spoon to my mouth.

"Luke, I am a submissive."

I coughed out a laugh, and along with it came half of the yogurt. After wiping the chunks of yogurt from my legs, the couch, and my shorts, I cocked an eyebrow and cleared my throat.

"Liv, stop pacing!" I demanded.

She stopped.

I motioned to the couch beside me. "Sit down."

She sat down on the opposite end of the couch. Although her hair was in complete contrast to her studded leather fuck-me-necklace, it looked elegant nonetheless. With her hands placed on each knee and her eyes fixed straight ahead, she sat in a statuesque pose. I studied her. She looked quite beautiful. The studded leather, attitude, labeling me Sir, and her claim of being a submissive meant someone or something convinced her she was submissive.

I gave an exaggerated sigh, finished my yogurt, and turned to face her.

"Spill it," I said dryly.

She reached up and delicately tapped the bun with her palm. "What?"

"Stop the act, you little weirdo. What is going on? And why are you wearing that strap on your neck?"

"It's a collar," she said in a matter-of-fact tone.

"Like a dog?"

"No, like a submissive."

"Who have you been talking to?"

"I don't need to talk to anyone to embrace who I truly am."

I cleared my throat. "Liv, have you talked to anyone about what we've been doing?"

With her hands still on her knees, she stared straight ahead. After a short moment, she turned her head to the side and made eye contact with me.

I glared back at her.

She lowered her head. "Yes."

"Who?"

She sighed. "Chloe."

"The girl you said was a slut? The one you called the other day?"

"Uh huh."

"And she told you that you were a submissive?"

"No." She pressed her forearms against her thighs and slumped forward. "I took a test."

I stood up, peered down at her, and shook my head. "At the submissive school?"

I walked to the kitchen, tossed my yogurt container into the trash, and placed my spoon in the dishwasher. As I walked into the living room, I began to chuckle at the thought of her state of mind.

There were many things that made Liv attractive to me. The biggest one was that Liv was just Liv. Sitting on the couch with her shoulders slumped and her mouth in full pout mode, the studded leather collar looked slightly more out of place.

But, all things considered, she was adorable.

I sat down on the couch beside her and rested my hand on her thigh. "What happened, Liv? Who gave you the test?"

She sighed. "I took it on the internet."

I fought not to laugh. "The submissive test?"

She nodded. "Uh huh."

"And the results said you were submissive?"

She sat up from her slumped position and cleared her throat. "It said I was 88% submissive. So I did some research. In the last two weeks I've read a ton of stuff. I'm definitely submissive."

"Interesting. And you took your test and did your reading on the internet?"

She raised her hands between us and began to plead her case. "I know what you're going to say, but there's so much information out there, and it's really easy to access it. Everything on the internet isn't garbage."

Since high school, I hadn't so much as turned a computer on. I didn't own one, wouldn't use one, and truly believed as useful as they were for many things, that they had become a huge contributor to the downfall of society.

"Okay, just for the sake of saying it, let's say your internet research is spot-on. Tell me how that changes things between us."

"Well, I'd say it lets me embrace my true self. I realize why I am the way I am. Why I like it when you do what you do to me, and why I have some of the desires I do." She raised her finger in the air. "Oh, and knowledge is power."

"So you feel empowered?"

"I do," she said with a nod.

"Take off that collar and I might listen to what you have to say."

She unsnapped the collar and formed it around her thigh. As she played with the silver studs, I considered her newfound knowledge and feelings of empowerment.

I had a pretty good idea on what caused me to be the way I was – at least from a sexual standpoint. Although I was anxious to find out what she felt she learned about herself through the course of her research, I was reluctant to ask for fear of her asking me the same question.

Eventually my curiosity won the struggle.

"So, why are you the way you are?"

After asking the question, I realized a small part of me wanted her to pry into my inner workings. To ask questions. To search for answers. She turned toward me and locked her eyes on mine. I braced myself for the inevitable. With her face begging for my acceptance, and her eyes filled with sincerity, she sighed lightly.

"I want to please you," she said.

Her response was much more satisfying to me than if she had pried. I returned her gaze and swallowed hard. I hadn't done any research or read any information regarding submissive behaviors on the internet, but somehow I felt I already knew the answer to the question I felt compelled to ask.

I asked anyway. "Why?"

"Honestly?" she asked.

I swallowed hard again. "Yes, honestly."

She chewed against the inside of her lip and lowered her head slightly. I lifted my cupped hand against her chin until her eyes met mine.

She released her lip. "Because I love you."

Her response filled me completely. In being entirely honest with myself, I had spent years loving Liv, yet fought against the urge to act on my feelings for fear of losing her. Our current arrangement initially provided me with a sense of security, but as time passed I felt I needed more. Feelings of selfishness, however, prevented me from even admitting how I felt.

Now, I felt the gate had been opened.

I felt consumed by the love I felt for her. Warmth washed over me. I turned to face her fully, swallowed heavily, and opened my arms. The words rushed from my mouth.

"I love you, too."

She all but collapsed into my arms. Holding herself tight against me, she brushed her cheek past mine and breathed against my neck.

"Finally," she whispered.

Apparently, I wasn't the only one who had been suppressing my feelings.

In each other's arms, we swayed back and forth without speaking. We didn't need to. At that moment, I was completely content, and no spoken word could have satisfied me more. After an immeasurable amount of time, I eventually felt a need to speak, but it was more out of excitement than out of necessity.

"You want to please me?" I asked.

She nestled her face into my neck. "Mmhhmm."

"I'm happier than I have ever been," I whispered.

She lifted her head slightly. "Because?"

"Because of you," I responded.

Because of you.

CHAPTER THIRTEEN

LIV

It had been two weeks since I told Luke I loved him. I came to realize pleasing Luke wasn't something that could be conquered. As far as I was concerned. It was it was an ongoing process. It may have had a beginning, but it had no ending. I felt an overwhelming desire to please him with everything I did. The look in his eyes, the way he responded, or the smile on his face had always been enough, but as the days progressed, I wanted him to be satisfied with everything from my choice of clothes to what I chose to cook for dinner.

The more I researched the characteristics of subservient women, the easier it was for me to accept that being submissive wasn't a choice I made. Right or wrong, I quickly decided I was naturally submissive. After doing so, my life began to make sense. My failed relationships, although probably destined to fail regardless due to my love for Luke, were all lacking in the areas where Luke and I flourished. Not only was I in love with Luke, I was in love with what he provided me.

Reassurance that who I was and what I was doing was exactly what he wanted and needed out of life.

"What the fuck is it?"

"A spiralizer," I said over my shoulder.

"And it makes noodles?"

"Kind of," I responded as I picked up a zucchini. "Out of veggies."

I had purchased the device at Williams Sonoma, hoping to be able to cook meals that made Luke happy. He liked to eat healthily, and although he wasn't one to watch his weight, he certainly paid attention to what he ate. Noodles made his feel bloated when he surfed, and although he loved the way they tasted, he refused to eat them for that reason.

Personally, I didn't want to eat pasta because it stuck with me for hours, and all we seemed to do after eating heavy meals was lay on the couch and moan for the entire evening. In short, there was no time for us to fuck after eating a big meal.

"Look!" I shouted as I turned the crank.

Zucchini noodles slightly larger than spaghetti came out the end of the machine. I watched in amazement as the length of squash disappeared on one side and the bowl filled with noodles on the other.

He wrapped his arms around my waist and rested his chin on my shoulder. I leaned to the side and kissed his cheek as he peered down at the bowl. "You're turning a zucchini into noodles?"

I nodded eagerly as the last bit of the spiralized squash fell into the bowl. "It's as easy as that."

"Right on," he said. "Now what?"

"I'm going to cook 'em in a skillet and we'll eat them with some spaghetti sauce," I said.

"Zucchini spaghetti?"

"Just wait and see, I bet you like it," I said.

He shrugged, walked to the refrigerator, and removed a container of yogurt.

Pessimist.

I transferred the noodles from the bowl to the skillet and tossed my head toward the doorway. "Go wait in the living room. Listen to music or something."

I heard The Cotton Jones Basket Ride's "Chewing Gum" began to play as I sautéed the noodles. The song was released the year we graduated high school and reminded me of the summer that followed. Luke was still in his relationship with Valerie, but I spent the summer single. As Valerie worked all day for the three-month break from school, Luke and I spent the summer together at the beach.

During that entire summer I felt guilty for being with Luke when he was committed to Valerie, but now I felt no guilt whatsoever. In hindsight, maybe the guilt was a result of my love for Luke – something I wasn't prepared to admit at the time.

"What does that song remind you of?" I asked over my shoulder as I stirred the sauce.

"Summer of 2008," he responded.

"Great summer," I shouted.

"Not as good as this one."

I checked the noodles, added a clove of garlic, and nodded my head. "I agree."

Cooking was something I enjoyed doing, but having someone to cook for seemed to make all the difference it he world. As the noodles became translucent I pulled the skillet from the stove, divided the zucchini onto the plates and ladled sauce over the top. A quick check of the oven's times showed one-minute left.

Perfect.

Small things seemed to satisfy me. Having the noodles done at the exact same time the chicken was ready was something I was trying to do, but accomplishing it made me smile. After removing the chicken from the oven and carefully placing one of the breasts on his plate, I shouted into the other room.

"It's ready!"

I walked to the table, placed the plates beside the bowls of salad, and admired the meal. As I noticed him walk into the kitchen, I turned and ran to the cupboard and pulled the silverware drawer open.

I playfully pushed him aside as he walked to his chair and set the knife and fork down beside his plate.

"There. Now, it's ready."

"Looks good." He inhaled a long breath through his nose, wagged his eyebrows and sat down. "Smells good."

Luke was like a grumpy old man in many respects. Set in his ways, and not willing to try new things or accept change, he often turned his nose up to things I was sure he would enjoy if he simply gave them a try. It wasn't limited to food, either.

He wasn't willing to accept or even discuss subtle changes regarding his clothes, food, beliefs in technology or music. He liked what he liked and he believed what he believed. It was just who Luke was. My preparation of the meal took tremendous guts on my part, and was a huge risk.

I rested my wrist on the edge of the table and watched as he raised the noodle-filled fork to his mouth. As he began to chew, I held my breath in wait.

And?

"God damn..." he said over his mouthful of food.

Good god damn, or bad god damn?

He swallowed.

"This is fucking awesome."

Yes!

I lowered my fork to my plate and grinned as I twisted the tines through the noodles. Seeing Luke satisfied with something I had done filled me with pride. It seemed strange, but I got more pleasure out of cooking a meal for him and having him express his approval than I did out of almost anything else I did in life.

With my eyes fixed on my plate, I fought to hide my excitement. "You like it?"

"Love it. It's like eating spaghetti without eating spaghetti. You know how bloated I feel the next day after eating pasta, right?"

That's exactly why I made it, Luke.

"Yeah, I kind if remember you saying that."

"Well, this is fucking awesome. It's noodles, but it isn't. Where'd you get that thing?"

"Williams Sonoma."

"Is it something new?" He shoveled another fork full of noodles into his mouth.

I shrugged. I didn't have the heart to tell him I had learned about it on Pinterest. If I had, he probably would have stopped eating.

"I don't know, I just saw it in there and thought you might like something healthy."

"Well, I don't care if this shit's going to kill me." He pointed thee tip of his fork at his plate. "I'd keep eating it. It's fucking goodness."

He took another bite, a huge one this time, smearing sauce on both corners of his mouth.

In his own strange way, Luke paid me a huge compliment, and he didn't even know it. After we ate, there was no doubt he would tell me he enjoyed the meal. As always, he'd thank me, tell me he liked it, and he'd help with the dishes.

Seeing the genuine excitement in his eyes and his eager appetite, however, was enough to let me know I was pleasing him in more ways than providing him with a wet pussy, a willing mouth, and a wayward mind.

We finished the meal, washed the dishes, and made a pot of coffee. While stirring my coffee, Luke raised his shirt, slapped his open hand against his washboard abs, and grinned. "I'm full, but I feel great. Hell, by the time we're done with this coffee, I'll be ready to fuck. That'd never happen with pasta, that's for sure."

I nodded and raised my cup of coffee as if toasting the suggestion.

The thought never crossed my mind.

CHAPTER FOURTEEN

LUKE

I shook my head and laughed to myself as he walked up the beach. After spending a lifetime surfing in southern California, I could now make two claims without reservation.

One, I had never given anyone pointers on how to surf.

And two, I had never seen anyone who was a poorer surfer than Perry.

While talking to him in the shop, I learned his parents had divorced when he was young, and that his father was an abusive drunk. Almost the exact opposite of my upbringing, but with similar circumstances, I immediately felt a need to help him find an outlet for his frustrations. I felt if there was something I could do to make him a better surfer, and in turn allow him to do it more frequently and greater passion, I wanted to do just that.

"What do you think?"

"Well," I said. "I think you've got the right board. Now, this might sound a little rude, but it sure isn't meant to be."

He lowered the tail of his board into the sand. "Okay."

"Forget everything you think you know about surfing. And I mean everything."

He gazed down at his feet. "Okay."

"Listen. The waves are breaking on your right. You surf left forward, so your heels are pointing in the direction you want to go. You've got do dig those heels into that board," I said.

He glanced up and nodded.

"Have you ever smashed a soda can with your foot? You know, stomped on one to squash it in one stomp?"

"Yeah."

"Okay, that's how much force you want to dig those heels in with. Dig in like that, and that wave is going shove right back at ya." I extended my left arm. "Toss your left hand out and twist your upper body with it. Just like you're pointing in the direction you want to surf."

He grinned. "Okay."

"Have you ever ridden a skateboard?"

"Yeah," he said.

I nodded my head. "Same concept. Heels down, and the skateboard goes left. Toes down, and it goes right. Same thing happens here."

I reached for his board.

Holding the board in front of me, I slapped my hand against the front third of the board, right on top of one of the decals. "Left foot right *here.* Right foot behind it, about one and a half times the width of your shoulders."

"Okay," he said. "I'm really sorry I'm not any better than this."

"You will be," I said. "Catch the next four-footer and let's see how well you listen.

He paddled out and waited. Two waves passed, and he made no effort to catch them. His problem, at least from what I could see, wasn't that he was incapable of paddling fast enough to catch a wave, it was staying up on his board after he caught it. Probably nervous, and a little disappointed in himself, he floated for a good fifteen minutes in wait.

A small swell began to rise, and he raised his head slightly.

This one's gonna be perfect.

Paddle. Paddle. Paddle, you little fucker.

Get it.

He got up, and immediately spread his feet and bent his knees. His foot placement was good, and the wave was breaking to his right.

Swing your body. Swing it…swing it…hand out…

His board swung left and along with it his upper body followed. It was the opposite of what I would have liked to see, but it was something we could work on if we needed to.

Dig those heels in. Dig 'em. Dig 'em…

The board carved left. The wave, slightly larger than I expected it would be, was every bit of six foot tall.

He dipped his toes, took a hard right, and immediately carved another left. Without consciously thinking, I began to walk toward closer to the shore.

He swung his right arm and carved out another hard tight.

Stay out of that shoulder, that lip will…

Immediately before being overtaken by the lip and crushed into the tube, he carved left.

Fuck yeah. Stay up…stay up…

He continued to ride until what little whitewater was left had diminished into the beach.

I pumped my fist in the air and shouted. "Fuck yeah!"

I felt a wave crash into me. Confused, I glanced down. Apparently, out of my sheer excitement to see Perry improve, I had managed to wade out into the ocean without even realizing it.

Out of breath and covered in a prideful grin, he stepped to my side. "I forgot everything and did exactly what you said."

"And it showed. Remember, look the direction you're surfing first, point your arm and body second, and transfer your weight last."

"Head, shoulders, feet," he responded.

"Exactly," I said.

"Have you got time for one more," he asked excitedly.

"I've got all day."

"You going to go up and get your board?" he asked.

"No. I'm going to teach you to surf."

His eyes widened and he hoisted his board under his arm. "How long can you stay?"

"How long do you think you can you surf?"

He grinned. "All day."

"All day it is."

The morning quickly faded into the afternoon, and before I knew it, the sun was low in the sky. Perry was showing no signs of exhaustion, and it was refreshing to see someone as eager as he was to learn, have the ability to apply himself, and make improvements with such speed.

"How's he doing?" I heard Liv's voice ask from behind me.

Shit.

I turned around. Dressed in jean shorts, flip-flops, and a white sleeveless button down top, she looked adorable. After admiring her for a moment, I alternated glanced between her and the ocean. "I think we're about done. What time is it?"

"A little after seven," she said.

"Shit, I'm sorry. I had no idea it was so late."

She shook her head and grinned. "I like it that you're teaching him to surf."

"Why's that?" I asked.

"How many people have you given surfing lessons to?"

I shrugged. "Hard to say."

"Give me an educated guess." She said with a laugh.

"None?"

"That's right. None," she said. "How many people have asked you to teach them?"

I chuckled. "Quite a few."

She tossed her head toward the shore. "What makes him different?"

"I don't know." I draped my arm over her shoulder and pulled her to my side.

"Maybe it's you."

I looked down the bridge of my nose at her. "Maybe it's me what?"

"Maybe it's you that's different. Maybe you've changed," she said.

I turned toward her and wrinkled my brow. "Maybe you're full of shit."

"Oh wow." She pointed toward the shore. "He's really doing good."

I turned toward the ocean and shielded the sun form my eyes. Perry had all but mastered the front side carve, and from where we were standing he looked like he had been surfing for a lifetime.

I pursed my lips and nodded.

"Front side carve?" she asked.

"That's exactly what it is," I said. "You should have seen him this morning."

"What did he do?"

"Nothing. He was awful. I told him to forget everything he thought he knew, and we'd go from there."

She turned to face me. "And he went from awful to that in one day?"

"One long day."

"Is that the board you made for him?" she asked.

I nodded my head. "Yep."

"Another grand," she said.

I shrugged. "Not exactly."

"Nine?"

"Not quite."

"Eight?"

I shook my head. "Nope."

"Seven? You didn't make a custom for seven, did you? Luke?"

I shook my head. "Nope."

"Less?"

I nodded. "A little less, yeah."

Liv knew my father gave me the shop after I graduated high school, and she further knew I had no rent to pay. The only thing I needed money for were utilities and food, and she fed me more than I ate at home. She had also been around me and the shop long enough that she knew exactly what I charged for a custom board.

"Six? You made a custom for six hundred bucks?"

I pointed toward the horizon. "Sure did. And a damned good one."

Perry was right underneath the lip, riding half way up the face of the wave. Three feet to his right, and he would have been in the tube, a surfers dream.

"He looks like he's doing great," she said.

"Big improvement over this morning."

As Perry waded through the water and toward the shore, I gazed beyond him and along the horizon. I really didn't have a reason for giving him a break on the board. At the time, I had no idea of his parent's divorce, and I sure didn't feel sorry for him.

As Perry stepped in front of us, drove the nose of his board into the sane and grinned. I returned his smile.

Liv was right. Something *had* changed.

The man in front of me was getting surfing lessons from someone who swore he'd never give them. The woman at my side was my life long best friend. For fear of losing her, I vowed to never be in a relationship with her.

But I was giving surfing lessons and I was in a relationship with Liv.

"Worn out?" I asked.

He nodded. "Long day."

"Perry, this is my girlfriend, Liv. Liv this is Perry."

"Nice to meet you," he said.

Liv grinned. "Nice to meet you. You looked great out there."

He slapped his hand against his board. "Luke Eagan custom and Luke Eagan lessons. I'm on top of the world."

"Shhh. Don't tell anybody."

"I won't."

"I tell you what," he said. "I'm starving. If you two want, I'll buy dinner. There's a great place right up here off the boardwalk on Mission Beach Boulevard. It's about two blocks down. It has great pasta."

Liv turned to face me and raised her eyebrows.

I nodded my head toward Perry. "Pasta sounds great."

As we turned away and began to walk toward the boardwalk, Perry followed close behind. Halfway up the beach, Liv slapped her hand against my ass. I glanced at her and narrowed my eyes jokingly.

"You delirious? Have a fever or something?" she asked.

"Not exactly," I said. "But kind of."

"What does that mean?"

I grinned and pulled her against me. "I'm in love. It's kind of like being sick and delirious at the same time."

"I know exactly what you mean," she said. "Today I went into the men's restroom."

"Piss in the urinal?"

She shook her head and laughed. "No, but I have a question."

I stepped on the boardwalk, kicked the sand from my feet, and turned to face her. "Okay."

"Your dick is so long," she whispered. "How do you pee in that thing without getting the tip of it all wet?"

"I can't tell you, it's a secret. A man thing."

She turned toward me, cocked her hip to the side, and eyed me up and down. "Uhhm, we don't keep secrets. A relationship won't ever work if there's secrets. So no secrets, okay?"

"Okay," I said, but not being completely truthful.

There was one more secret I had kept from her – from everyone – for my entire life. I knew one day I'd have to tell her; but as much as felt I wanted to, I continued to tell myself I was simply waiting for the right time.

I knew, however, there would never be a time suitable for such a horrid tale.

CHAPTER FIFTEEN

LIV

Living in San Diego ended up being a blessing. With people ten times weirder than me in any direction, it was easy to dismiss myself and my desires to normal behavior. Southern California was a unique mixture of people, styles, cultures, beliefs, and theories.

I lived in a melting pot.

And, for once in my life, I was grateful to be surrounded by the eclectic mixture of people the city offered.

"Mondays, Wednesdays, and Fridays," Chloe said.

I chewed the inside of my lip. "Because you want to or you have to?"

"I don't *have* to do a god damned thing. It's my *choice*." After a short pause, she laughed. "Well, kind of."

"Oh my god. It's Wednesday. Is it?" My eyes fell to her waist.

"Yep." She nodded. "Sure is."

"So." The thought of it made me slightly uncomfortable. "What's it like?"

"I don't know." She shrugged. "A reminder. It's sensual. It's kind of like. I don't know. I feel filled up. And it's a great prep for anal. I'm guessing you've never been fucked in the ass, huh?"

I shook my head. "Uhhm, no. Does it. Does it, uhhm. Does it hurt?"

Or conversation eventually migrated from submissive women to her wearing a butt plug three days a week. It seemed the more I got to know about Chloe, the guiltier I felt for feeling the way I felt about her for years. I had always perceived her as a slut, but now believed I had more in common with her than any other girl I knew.

"It could if some idiot is doing it. Personally, I love it. I think every woman would it if they were with the right guy."

"So, do you…do you…you know. Do you have an orgasm from it?" I asked.

She laughed out loud. When she finally caught her breath, she studied me. The look on my face must have given it away.

Her eyes narrowed. "You're serious, aren't you?"

I shrugged. "Sorry."

"The orgasms are intense. It's hard to explain. Yeah." She chuckled. "Orgasms galore."

"Huh," I said. "Never would have guessed it."

"You need to have Luke do it. But, do some research first. You'll need to prepare yourself, and go slow. Start small and work your way up to it."

"Is it, you know, messy?"

She laughed again. "No."

"Oh. It's just. I would have thought…"

"Just try it. It's not what you're thinking. Maybe you'll like it, maybe you'll hate it," she said. "There's only one way to find out. How big is Luke's cock?"

It was my turn to laugh, and I did for some time. When I finally stopped, I placed the edges of my palms against the table and spread them apart until it looked like the space between them was about as far as the length of Luke's dick.

She glanced down at my hands and shifted her eyes to meet mine. It appeared she was shocked.

"Seriously?"

I glanced down at my hands. It looked a little short. I moved them apart another inch or so. I nodded my head toward my hands. "Like that."

Her eyes fell to my hands.

"Thick?" she asked.

I glanced at my wrist. I'd made mental comparisons between my wrist and his cock before. As I sat and studied it, the more I similar they seemed in size. I clasped my left hand around my right wrist. The size was about perfect.

"I've got small wrists, but yeah. About like that."

She swallowed hard. "You're serious? His cock is as thick as your wrist?"

I nodded. "Uhhm. Yeah, pretty much."

"Show me a picture."

I shrugged. "I don't have one."

"Liar."

"Seriously, I don't."

"Every good subbie has a pic of their man's cock," she said with a laugh.

I had one, but I didn't want to show her. I'd taken several pictures of Luke with his shirt off, and although he wasn't initially thrilled about it, he eventually agreed to a few naked pics. I wanted to show her, because I wanted Luke's cock to be bigger and better than Kavin's, but it didn't seem right to do so. Personally, I loved having them on my phone, but sharing them seemed slutty.

"Actually, I've got one, but…I don't know, it seems weird."

"Just show me," she sighed.

I wrinkled my nose. "Why?"

"Because," she said. "I want to see it. It's a cock. It's no big deal. I mean, we're sitting here talking about butt sex."

She had a good point. I pulled my phone from my purse, scrolled through the pictures, and found one where he was fully erect. After zooming in on his waist area and cropping the rest of the photo out, I saved the pic and handed her my phone.

"Jesus," she gasped.

I grinned. "I know, right?"

She stared down at my phone for some time eventually turning it to face me. "I like this one." A picture of Luke with his cock in his hand, naked from head to toe, was on the screen.

"You skank," I said as I reached for my phone.

She laughed. "It's just hard to put in perspective without something else in the picture, sorry. He's freaking hung, isn't he?"

It seemed odd, but I felt prideful hearing her say Luke was hung. Maybe her acceptance meant more to me due to her vast knowledge of everything kinky. I grinned and put my phone back in my purse.

I reached for my beer. "Yeah."

"Big cocks rule," she said.

I raised my glass of beer, nodded, and tilted it toward her. "Amen, Sister."

"Now, when he fucks you in the ass with that thing," she said as she raised her glass. "Take it slow and easy, or he'll rip you open."

My eyes widened. "Seriously?"

She coughed out a laugh and nodded as she raised the glass to her lips. "Yeah, seriously. Just start out small and work your way up to it."

I crossed my legs, uncrossed them, and fidgeted in my seat a little. "We'll see."

She grinned. "You're thinking about it right now."

She was right. I was, and thinking about it had me hornier than hell. I had always considered myself to be horny, but after Luke and I were truthful about our love for each other, it seemed I couldn't stop thinking about sex. The timing of me admitting I was submissive coming at the same time may have had something to do about it, but I wasn't sure. The only thing that I was certain about was that I seemed to be a walking orgasm waiting for a little stimulation.

"Are you horny all the time?" I asked.

"Twenty-four seven."

"Really?"

"Yeah, really," she said.

"I don't feel so bad, then."

"You know," she said. "People are born addicted to drugs or alcoholics or whatever. Their chemical make-up. It's off. And as soon as they try a drink or like smoke a bowl, they're fucked. Hooked for life. As long as they never try it, they never know. Little sluts like us with an insatiable sexual appetite just need a man capable of satisfying us, and we're like a morphine addict waiting at the clinic for his next shot."

"I can go without sex."

"Really?" she waved her hand toward my purse. "Even now that you've had *that* cock."

I nodded. "Yep."

"Okay," she said. "Two weeks. Go without that cock for two weeks."

"I don't want to."

She laughed. "You can't. Shit, I bet you can't go a week."

"I most certainly can.'"

"Prove it."

It was ridiculous. I didn't need to prove anything to her, but there was no way I was addicted to sex or Luke's cock. I had gone months without sex, and going a week was absolutely nothing.

"Fine," I said.

"No dick whatsoever," she said.

"None."

She clenched her fist and held it over the center of the table. I looked at it, glanced at her, and wrinkled my nose.

She nodded toward her hand. "Pound it."

"Oh." I giggled.

I pounded my fist against hers and grinned.

Chloe had somehow transformed from some slut I went to school with to being my sexual mentor, and I was grateful for the change.

"Honor system," she said. "You've got to be truthful."

"Okay."

No sex for one week. No problem. All I had to do was convince Luke to focus on other things.

It seemed lately all he enjoyed was surfing, spending time with me, and fucking.

There was no fucking way I was going to make it.

CHAPTER SIXTEEN

LUKE

Liv had been crossing, re-crossing, and adjusting her legs repeatedly the entire night. What little time she wasn't nervously fidgeting in her seat, she had spent daintily walking back and forth to the kitchen. For the life of me I couldn't figure out what was wrong, so I finally decided to just say *something*.

She narrowed her lips and squinted as she pressed her palms against her thighs.

I leaned away from her and stared. "You seem nervous."

"I'm fine."

"Is your stomach bothering you?"

She grinned. "No."

"Something's wrong."

She wiggled her hips back and forth, forcing herself deeper into the cushion. "No, everything's fine."

"You've been wiggling all over the couch since this show started."

I didn't watch television, and since moving out of my father's home immediately following high school, hadn't even owned a television. From time to time, however, Liv and I enjoyed a movie on Netflix or Hulu. This particular attempt at doing so seemed to be a bust.

"Just trying to get comfortable."

I exchanged glances between the T.V. and Liv. "What's keeping you from it?"

"From what?"

"Form getting fucking comfortable," I said. "When I was a kid and my sister used to wiggle around like that, my dad would say it looked like she had ants in her pants. That's what it looks like."

"I uhhm. I'm just…" She uncrossed her legs and quickly crossed them again.

I leaned away from her and against the arm of the couch. She stopped wiggling, glanced at me, and quickly looked away.

"Spill it," I demanded.

She looked like the cat who had just eaten the canary. "What?"

I reached for the remote, turned off the television, and glared at her. "What in the fuck is going on?"

She sighed. "I swear. I can't keep anything from you."

"I thought we agreed there'd be no secrets."

"We did," she said. "I wasn't keeping a secret. I mean, not really. Eventually I was going to say something."

"Well, what's the secret you weren't really keeping from me?"

She stood and slowly walked toward the kitchen. Her manner of walking was different. She no longer strolled along with the grace of a runway model – she looked more like her butt was chafed and she was trying to keep her ass cheeks from rubbing together.

Half the distance to the kitchen doorway, she stopped and turned to face me. She looked like she was walking on broken glass. Barefoot.

"I uhhm. Well, you know Chloe and I went to lunch. And, well, we were talking," he said.

I tossed my left arm over the back of the couch, slumped into the seat, and craned my neck toward her. "I'm listening. I can't wait to see where this goes."

"Well, this might sound crazy at first, but it's actually not *that* crazy. I mean not really."

"Spill it, Liv."

She sighed. "I'm just going to come out and say it, then we can talk about it."

I glared. In the middle of me taking a breath, she continued.

"I've got a butt plug poked in my butt right now," she blurted.

I coughed half the air out of my lungs, choked, and laughed until my eyes watered. "What?"

She smiled innocently and shrugged. "I know. I told you it'd sound crazy, but really it's not."

I caught my breath, stood from the couch, and folded my arms in front of my chest. Her and Chloe's definition of sanity and mine were apparently much different.

"You have a rubber plug in your ass right now?"

The innocent smile returned.

"You get one of the big ones?" I laughed.

"No!" she snapped back. "The one I'm on now is medium-sized."

I chuckled. She was adorable. Her discovery of her true sexual self was an entertaining feat to witness, but keeping from laughing during the process was proving to be quite difficult.

"Now? Medium-sized?"

She wagged her knees back and forth and twisted her hips. "I got a kit. There's three of 'em in it. I'm on the middle one now."

I pointed at her knees and grinned. "Looks like it might be a little bit too big for you, huh?"

"No."

I chuckled. "You look a little uncomfortable."

She shook her head. "I'm not. I'm just really horny."

"Simple fix, Liv. Let's fuck."

Guilt seemed to wash over her. Her mouth went into a full pout and her eyes fell to the floor.

"What?"

"I can't. I bet Chloe I could go a week without fucking you," she murmured.

I uncrossed my arms and pressed my hands against my hips. "You *what*?"

She nodded. "A week."

"You two need to be separated. She's a bad influence. What did you bet?"

"Like how much money or whatever?" she asked.

"Yeah. What was the wager?"

"Uhhm. We just bet. Like a bet. No money or anything."

"Lose the bet." I shrugged. "You're not out anything."

She pressed her hands into her thighs and bent slightly at the waist. "I don't want to lose; I want to win."

"Fine," I said, tossing my hand toward her. "What day are you on now?"

"Two," she said. "Well, if we include the day we made the bet."

"When did you make it?"

She swiveled her hips a little more and apparently found just what she was looking for. The corners of her mouth curled into a smile. "Yesterday."

I laughed out loud. "Yesterday? You're on day *one*. You haven't even made it one day?"

She rubbed her palms up and down the length of her thighs as her knees knocked into each other. "Do you know anything about anal sex?"

Valerie and I had anal sex a few times, and she didn't enjoy it at all. I didn't find her lack interest surprising considering the size of my cock. I enjoyed it immensely, but inductive reasoning convinced me it would be something Liv and I would never agree on.

"A little," I said with a laugh.

"This thing's diving me crazy," she said. "I want to try it."

"Six more days." I laughed.

"Fuck Chloe," she snapped back.

The thought excited me, but Liv was six days from a getting a green light. "Well, it's not that easy," I said. "We've got to get lube, and we've got to…"

"Got it," she interrupted.

I widened my eyes. "You've got the lube?"

"Yep."

"Well, I don't know what you've got for plugs, but we should really get some toys to tease you with and prep you for…"

She raised her hand and extended her index finger. "Got 'em."

I laughed. "Seems all we're down to is desire."

She unfastened her shorts, unzipped the zipper, and began forcing them down along her thighs.

After spending my entire life being friends with Liv, discovering we were sexually compatible was very comforting. Determining we had been in love with each other and were merely too afraid to admit it was even more reassuring. The most encouraging of all, however, was finding out Liv was as much or more of a sexual deviant than I was.

As I watched her, I grinned, wondering just what kind of trouble we were going to get ourselves into.

Whatever it was, I was prepared to find out.

CHAPTER SIXTEEN

LIV

No matter how uncomfortable I seemed to feel as a result of my odd sexual desires, Luke's acceptance of me was all the reassurance I needed. He made it obvious that although I may not fit into the world's mold of a typical 25-year-old woman, I snapped into place in his perfectly.

After an hour-long session of kissing, sucking his cock, vaginal intercourse, and experiencing having him tease my ass with various toys, I was mentally prepared for my introduction into the world of women who had tried butt sex.

"Please don't fuck me in the ass," I whined.

"I thought you wanted me to…"

I pressed my bare chest into the comforter, reached behind me, and spread my ass cheeks as wide as I could.

"You can fuck me, Mister. But, please. Whatever you do, don't shove your cock in ass."

I was done playing around. Knowing Luke had more hang-ups than I did, I thought maybe the *please don't fuck me, Mister* routine may coerce him into taking the next step.

Spreading my ass cheeks only made matters worse. For whatever reason, spreading my ass apart was turning me on. Hell, everything turned me on. As I felt Luke gathering my hair in his hand, I pressed my face into the comforter and prayed.

I felt cold lube on my ass. Something, but definitely not his cock, began sliding in and out of my ass. I sighed a shallow sigh of boredom into the comforter and although he couldn't even see me, rolled my eyes.

A few seconds later, and I felt his cock slide into my overly anxious pussy. We had exercised foreplay for so long my twat had opened up like a flower. The introduction of his cock into my wet crevice was like tossing a cucumber down the hallway. Two or three full strokes of his cock later, and I fought to convince myself that I was satisfied.

Quickly becoming bored with the thought of having him fuck me, and feeling terrible for harboring the feeling, I raised from the comforter slightly and leaned forward. Hoping to cause him to at least tug against my hair slightly, I was disappointed when I felt no resistance whatsoever.

He slowly slid himself out of my wetness.

I sighed, wondering if another session of me sucking his cock was next. Hopefully, if nothing else, I could convince him to fuck my face.

It would be better than nothing.

I felt slight pressure on my asshole as he pulled my hair tight. Then, a little more pressure against my ass. He forced his chest against my back as he lifted my head and shoulders by pulling my hair even more taught.

"Not in the ass, huh?" he breathed into my ear.

Oh, God. Please.

"No, please no!" I whimpered.

I felt his girth slowly slide inside of me.

Holy shit.

With great care, he worked himself in and out of my tight ass, giving me a little more length with each stroke. I chewed against my lip as I tried to identify just what it was I was feeling, knowing nothing more than the fact that I liked it. It was much different than being fucked in the pussy, but I was in heaven regardless. The feeling of cold lube against my ass startled me, but not near as much as what followed.

I clenched the comforter in my hands and gasped as he slid his entire length into me. I tried to collapse into the comforter only to have him pull against my hair and breathe his warm breath into my ear.

"Too bad I don't let little girls call the shots," he growled.

Apparently all of the anal foreplay was for good reason. Without further warning, he began to work his girth in and out of my ass. My eyes bulged and I opened my mouth wide, but for all the right reasons.

It was incredible.

Chloe was right.

Being fucked in the ass was everything I had hoped for.

And more.

He continued to fuck my ass deeply but not savagely. Confused on why I was enjoying it as much as I was, I simply exhaled what little breath I had left in my lungs and allowed myself to relish in the odd sensuality of having Luke balls-deep inside my ass.

With his muscular forearm pressed into my upper back and my hair clenched in his fist, he gripped my neck with his free hand. Now pulling against the front of my neck and squeezing it slightly, he had me on the verge of what was undoubtedly going to be the most intense orgasm I ever had the luxury of experiencing.

"You sexy little bitch," he breathed into my ear. "I love that tight little ass of yours."

Jesusfuckingchrist.

He released my neck and continued to punish my virgin ass. As my mind continued to swim in the pool of sensual bliss anal sex had cast me into, I felt his finger slide deep into my pussy. Within a few seconds, he was finger fucking me into a complete state of confusion. My body, my mind, and two of my three available holes were all fighting for a means of expressing their pleasure. Realizing I was on the cusp of something earth shattering, I opened my mouth and waited for whatever it was to escape me.

He continued to simultaneously jackhammer his finger in and out of my twat and fuck my ass with the precision of a trained professional. And, just like that, he found my threshold.

As he methodically proceeded to tickle my g-spot with the tip of his middle finger and fuck my ass with the entire length of his throbbing cock, every muscle in my body tensed, released, and then began to quiver.

A mild groan escaped me.

Then, it evolved into a growl.

And with the growl came a sensual explosion.

"Ooooohhhhh." I moaned in a sixty-second-long blood-curdling howl.

From well within me, an orgasm of epic proportion unleashed. Unlike any other climax I had ever experienced, it came from deep inside of me and not from my outer extremities. I opened my eyes wide and let it flow through me like a sexual river rushing to its final destination.

My ears rang, my vision blurred, and the two holes that were filled with Luke's love felt like they exploded at the same time.

Luke had once again hit spots in me I didn't even know I had. Fabulous sex had quickly been redefined.

I collapsed face-first onto the comforter. A few minutes later, and I found myself staring blankly at the ceiling, not necessarily knowing how I got there.

My legs were shaking ever-so-slightly, but uncontrollably.

"Come here, Baby," he said.

I blinked a few times and stared as he picked me up and into his arms.

"We're going to go take warm bath," he said.

Incapable of responding, I simply gazed up at him and nodded.

He provided me what I wanted, what I had begged for, and what I thought I needed, but on his own terms. I wasn't prepared for the intensity of the orgasm that followed, but I doubted anything I could have done would have prepared me.

Luke wasn't only my best friend, sexual partner, and lover.

He also protected me from myself without making me feel like an idiot.

And, for that reason alone, I loved him even more.

One orgasm at a time.

CHAPTER SEVENTEEN

LUKE

I had been in love with Liv since we were in high school, and although I never acted on my feelings, my love for her never escaped me. Based on my opinions of myself, I had made an effort to protect her from me – choosing to love her from afar. In the many years that followed, I felt the depth of my love slowly diminishing until it was something I was comfortable living with. In looking back on what I allowed myself to feel – and to express – I realized not only was I protecting Liv, I was attempting to protect myself.

Now loving her without limitations or reservation, it seemed that nothing else mattered in my life. Surfing had not become unimportant, but it certainly wasn't on the forefront of my preferred leisure activities. My midnight strolls along the beach turned into uninterrupted nights of dreamless sleep.

My life had become the opposite of what I had spent a lifetime fearing.

She buckled her seatbelt, glanced at me, and exhaled. "My mom and dad rode this thing when I was in kindergarten. I'm serious. Once, and then I'm done."

She agreed to ride the rollercoaster at my insistence, but with great reluctance. As long as the amusement park had been in service, it saddened me that she had never taken the time to ride Mission Beach's oldest attraction. The fact I was busting her rollercoaster cherry made up for it, though.

"Once is fine," I said. "Listen to this. My father's father's father not only ride this fucker with his wife, he rode it when he was a little kid."

She peered over the edge of the car and down along the wooden structure.

"Yeah, my great grandfather," I said. "When he was little, in like 1935. And he said back then it was already an *old* amusement park. Every generation of my family from then until now has ridden this fucker with their wife."

The attendant checked everyone's seatbelt, and after giving instructions regarding remaining seated in our cars, started the ride. One of the world's oldest rollercoasters, and one of few remaining wooden rollercoasters in the United States, Belmont Park's *The Big Dipper* was an attraction I had spent a lifetime enjoying.

As the car slowly clanked along the tracks, she gazed over the edge of the ride. "I'm scared."

"Don't be," I said. "We haven't even gone up the first hill yet. And remember, this thing only flies off the tracks like, I don't know, maybe once a year."

"Luke, stop it. I swear."

As we slowly climbed the last few feet to crest of the first hill I raised my hands high it the air.

"She said leave your hands in the car."

I cocked an eyebrow as the car reached the top.

Liv raised her hands above her head.

The car reached the apex, seemed to pause for a second, and then plummeted to the bottom of the tracks.

A shrill scream escaped Liv's lungs.

The car shot up the next hill, slowing slightly toward the top, only to quickly fall again. The process repeated itself over and over, all but extracting the air from our lungs each time. After coming to a stop back where we originally started, Liv sighed and turned to face me.

I had a feeling she actually enjoyed herself.

"Let's do it again," she said.

"I told you that you'd like it."

"I didn't say I liked it. I said I wanted to go again."

I shrugged and laughed lightly. "Okay."

Five rollercoaster rides and two hours later, it was apparent she learned a little but about her sense of adventure.

"I want an ice cream cone," she said.

Ice cream wasn't something I typically ate. As far as I was concerned, yogurt was a treat.

I grinned and nodded. "Sounds great."

As we buried our faces into two of the largest ice cream cones I had ever seen, we laughed, talked about when we were kids, and agreed that we had been deeply in love with each other since we first met. And, for the first time since I was a young child, my life felt like it was finally in order.

I eagerly nibbled the last few bites of my waffle cone from my sticky fingertips. "Okay, this isn't something I want to do every day, but that motherfucker was *good*."

Liv's cone looked like it did when they handed it to her. She was adorable. Sitting on the stool in her raggedy jean shorts with her legs crossed and her elbow resting on her knee, she held the cone directly in front of her face, savoring it one lick at a time. Obviously unaware of my interest, she forced her tongue against the chocolate ice cream, leaving a beveled path along the surface.

She glanced up. Chocolate ice cream covered the corners of her mouth. "I love ice cream."

"I didn't know I did, but I guess I do."

Her eyes darted around me. "Where's yours?"

"Gone," I said.

She extended her arm. "Wanna lick?"

I grinned. "No, you go right ahead. I'm having fun watching you."

She wrinkled her nose. "Weirdo."

We both seemed shocked by her phone ringing, and as she pulled it from her purse, I instinctively pressed my hands against my shorts and realized my phone, as always, wasn't with me. Most people's crutch, and my personal annoyance, a cell phone was something I felt I needed to have but rarely used.

"Uhhm, it's your dad," she said, her voice conveying the emotion she was feeling.

She handed me the phone. "There's been an accident."

As I accepted the phone, she tossed her ice cream into trash and grabbed her purse.

"Your brother's been hit by a car," my father said.

My mouth immediately went dry. I tried to swallow, but my throat constricted. I wondered the worst, but quickly convinced myself that if he had been killed, my father would have said so already.

I swallowed hard. "Was he. Was he uhhm. On his bike?"

"Yeah. I've been trying to call you, but. Well, it doesn't matter. He's alive, Luke, but he's pretty banged up."

His voice faltered. He cleared his throat. "Both arms are broken. And. God damn it. His uhhm. His legs. The uhhm."

I fought against the emotion. "Pop?"

"I'm here," he said. "The car. His legs are shattered, Luke."

"Where is he?"

"Balboa. He's still in the emergency room. The trauma unit."

"We'll be there in fifteen," I said.

"Luke?"

"Yeah, Pop?"

"Drive careful, okay?"

"See you in fifteen."

Matthew was three years younger than me, and I felt as compelled to protect him as I did Liv. He was his own person, however, and lived a life not much differently than I did. Riding his bicycle was his salvation.

As we silently rode to the hospital, I wondered if he'd ever be able to ride it again, and if not, what would become of him.

The same thing, I guessed, that would become of me if I lost Liv.

CHAPTER EIGHTEEN

LIV

We stood in the small room with Luke's father and two sisters. From what the police officer had said, Matthew was riding along a bike path when a woman swerved out of her lane of traffic, running over him from behind. He was crushed by the car, breaking both arms, fracturing his skull, and shattering his legs.

Although the doctors weren't certain, there was little hope that he would ever walk again, let alone ride his bike. Bicycling was to Matthew what surfing was to Luke, and even though I was grateful he was alive, I felt terrible that something he loved as much as cycling would an activity he would never be able to enjoy again.

Still unconscious, and wrapped in bandages and casts from head-to-toe, what little portion of his face that was exposed was covered in cuts. There was no doubt he was lucky to be alive, but looking at him made it extremely difficult to find any good in what had happened.

I squeezed Luke's hand as he talked quietly with his father.

"How are you? I haven't seen you two in forever," I whispered to his sisters.

"Fine, just been busy with work," Sarah said. "Are you still doing the graphic artist stuff?"

I smiled and nodded. "Yeah."

I shifted my focus to Mary.

"I'm good. Married. And we're in San Clemente," she said.

Mary and Sarah were a year apart in age, and were three and four years older than Luke, respectively. Growing up, it seemed they were a pair of independent children apart from Luke and Matthew. The boys and the girls were oddly separated in pairs, each group treated differently by the parents. The girls spent all of their time at home, and the boys rarely went home unless forced to do so – Matthew spending his time on his bicycle, and Luke at the beach.

As much time as Luke and I spent together as kids, most of it was at my parent's house, and very rarely would we even go to his home. What little time we did spend there was generally for Luke to change clothes or get his surfboard.

An odd family that seemed to have no hatred toward one another, but certainly wasn't close-knit by any means, they didn't spend time together like most families. I spent more time with my parents, and they lived half a nation away.

Sad that an event like this had to bring everyone together, but grateful to see them all in one room, I stood and tried to smile as Luke asked questions about his brother's future. As he finished talking to his father, he exchanged awkward glances with his sisters and then pulled me close.

"He said we'll just have to wait and see," he whispered.

I forced a slight smile. "For right now, we should just be thankful he's alive."

He reached for what little portion of Matthew's fingers that extended beyond the end of the cast. As he gently cupped the palm of his hand around his brother's, he turned toward me and nodded. "I know."

The machine above Matthew's bed beeped at a steady pace, making the otherwise silent room seem to be occupied by something alive and willing to communicate with the entire family. As Luke spoke softly to his unconscious brother, I lowered my head and began to pray.

"Oh wow," I heard Mary gasp.

I turned around.

I hadn't seen her in years, and although she was considerably older, her dark complexion and almost black eyes made her unmistakable. I knew there were hard feelings between Luke and his mother, and as soon as I recognized her I wondered just how well they would get along.

My answer was immediate.

"What the fuck are you doing here?" Luke howled.

Sarah glanced toward Luke. "Luke!"

Luke pointed toward the door. "Get the fuck out!"

Her face seemed to fill with shame. She raised her hands slightly as if forming a buffer between them.

"Luke, I…" she began.

Luke's father lowered his head. "Ruth, I don't know that…"

Luke pulled his hand away from mine. Seeming almost overcome by emotion, he quickly stepped in front of her and placed his hands against her shoulders. She appeared on the verge of tears.

"Get the fuck out!" Luke demanded, pushing her toward the door slightly. "And don't you fucking dare come back."

She turned toward the door, paused, and walked out. Sarah and Mary followed, leaving Luke's father behind.

"Luke, I had no idea," his father said apologetically.

"Who the fuck told her?" Luke asked.

His father tilted his head toward the door. "I'm sure it was one of your sisters."

"If she comes back in here," Luke said. "I'll call the fucking cops. She has no right."

His father nodded. "I'll make sure she doesn't."

As his father turned toward the door, I reached for Luke's hand. As soon as my fingers touched his skin, he instinctively pulled away.

"Luke?"

"Sorry," he said. "I'm just. She. Come on, let's just go."

"You want to leave?" I asked.

"I *need* to," he responded.

I glanced at his brother, shifted my eyes back to Luke, and nodded. "Okay."

The ride to my house was eerily quiet. After we parked the car, Luke walked inside, went to the couch, and sat quietly for several hours.

I felt he may need time to think, so I left him alone and started dinner. When he refused to eat, I began to wonder. When he refused sex I wondered even more.

But it was when he pulled his knees to his chest and began humming while rocking back and forth that I became worried.

And, from there, things only got worse.

Much worse.

CHAPTER NINETEEN

LUKE

I finished the glass of bourbon and poured another two-ounce shot. With slight reluctance, I walked into the living room and sat down. As I sipped the whisky from the glass, I stared down at the baseboard and began to recite a portion of my childhood I had spent a lifetime attempting to forget.

"When we're kids, we've got this expectation of our parents protecting us. It doesn't matter if it's the bumping noises in the night or the toy in our closet that somehow casts a shadow that makes it look like an eight-foot tall monster. Whatever we're incapable of conquering, we've got this impression that our parents are not only able – but willing – to save us from the clutch of what it is that might harm us."

Out of my peripheral, saw Liv nod. I took a shallow sip and lowered the glass.

"Well," I said. "That isn't always the case. Or at least it wasn't at my house."

I raised the glass to my mouth, paused, and inhaled the aroma of the whisky. As my mouth began to salivate, I took another sip.

"I don't really remember it, but I do. It's hard to explain. I remember the guilt. Fuck. I was filled with guilt for so long. And then? After the guilt?"

I turned to face her. I don't really know what I expected her to do or say, but regardless, she sat at the end of the couch with her hands in her lap and stared back at me stone-faced.

I smiled a complacent smile, satisfied she was providing exactly what I needed to continue.

I shifted my eyes back to the baseboard. "After the guilt, I got angry. Every time it happened, I got mad. You know the funny thing?"

I took another short drink and winced at the taste. The question was rhetorical, and she knew it. I didn't need confirmation or an answer to continue, I only needed guts. This was a story I yearned to tell, but seemed rather reluctant to do so now that the time had come. If I could somehow find the courage to share it with someone, Liv would be that person.

I gazed blankly at the floor. "I wasn't mad at her. I was angry with myself. Somehow, at least at first, I told myself whatever she was doing was my fault. She said she did it to make me more focused. To make me have a better understanding of life. Life isn't easy. That's what she told me. *Life isn't easy.*"

I finished what little whisky remained and let the glass dangle from between my thumb and forefinger as I continued.

"So, she'd make me get my homework and study. And while I studied, she'd…you know…she'd uhhm…"

I glanced in her direction.

I needed her to tell me it was okay.

She reached for my hand. I forced a smile and returned the gesture, taking her hand in mine.

As we did so many times on the way home from school, we held hands. It was comforting. I sat for a long moment and somehow converted

Liv's energy to my own. As the warmth of her hand transferred to the surface of my palm, I found the nerve to continue.

"So, every night, or at least I think it was every night, she'd make me study my homework. And while I did, she'd uhhm..."

I fought against my tightening throat and swallowed. It wasn't easy to continue, but I knew I needed to.

"She'd touch me. Then, I'd uhhm…you know…I'd lose uhhm…I'd lose focus."

I took a glance in her direction and quickly shifted my focus to the floor. "That's what I was trying to say. I'd lose focus. And when I did, she'd scream at me. She told me when I reached a point that I didn't lose focus, we'd stop."

Her hand was shaking.

I turned toward her.

A tear escaped her eye and slowly worked its way down along her cheek. I hadn't realized it until I saw hers, but as I sat and watched it diminish as it rolled past the corner of her mouth, it came to me that I was crying as well.

I reached up and wiped my cheeks with the side of my finger.

She did the same.

"I don't really know when, but I finally reached a point when I was able to focus. You know, I graduated with honors, but I didn't go to college. Everyone wanted to know why. In hindsight, I think I was scared. You know, even though she had been gone for some time, it was still really tough for me to convince myself it was over. I was sure if for whatever reason I couldn't get good grades, she'd reappear and it'd all start over again."

I raised the glass to my lips and tipped the bottom up. After realizing it was empty, I lowered it into my lap and sighed.

"I was a pretty strong kid. You know, nobody knew anything. But Matt?"

I shook my head. "I was twelve at the time. I think I may have even told myself it didn't happen. You know, that it was all some kind of crazy dream or something. I think, to tell you the truth, I told myself it was what I deserved – or maybe what I needed. I remember thinking my good grades were a result of her persistence or whatever. But Matt?"

I clenched my jaw and shook my head. "I was twelve. I went to get my surfboard. You know, he was eight. Maybe he was nine, I don't know. And she was…"

I stood from the couch and realized she was still holding my hand in hers. I don't know where I was going, but wherever it was, Liv changed my mind. Without speaking, she pulled against my hand slightly and convinced me to sit down.

I inhaled a deep breath and exhaled until I was satisfied I was ready. "Her uuhm. Her head was in his lap."

Saying it frustrated me. I clenched my teeth and inhaled a long breath through my nose. "I lost it. I remember beating her until Matt ran out and got dad. He talked to each one of us after that. I think I may have blamed him a little bit, too. But it didn't last for long. It was all her."

"She was an evil bitch."

She pulled me into her, cupped her hand against my cheek, and guided my head onto her chest.

As I sat snuggled up against her, I relaxed to a point of weakness. I later realized it was exactly what I had been needing to allow myself to truly recover. For the few seconds that followed, however, I was embarrassed.

Until she joined me.

And, in each other's arms, we sat and cried until we were both incapable of shedding another tear.

CHAPTER TWENTY

LIV

Being kicked in the gut. That's all I could think of that would explain what I felt after Luke described what happened with his mother. I knew one day something would come along in life and knock me to my knees, but I had no idea it would be Luke revealing details of his mother's abuse of him as a child that did it.

Luke was in pain; therefore, I was in pain. I had been awake for most of the night, certain the aching in my soul would become a permanent part of my being. As hard as I tried, I couldn't make the images in my mind go away. Halfway through the sleepless night I decided I didn't want to know what happened to him. I wanted him to take it back. I wanted the thoughts, the ideas, the images, and the lingering sickening feeling to all go away. When we woke the next day, the morning we shared was awkward – I didn't know what to say, and apparently he had already said all he was capable of. He eventually left, seeking his comfort at the beach. I, in turn, called my office and explained I was far too sick to come in to work.

No one on this earth could ever convince me what his mother did was done with the belief that it was constructive. She was a sickening woman committing a sickening act for sickening reasons of self-gratification. I wanted her to be in jail or dead and as much as I knew

I should feel terrible for wishing that upon another person, I didn't. I hated her and I hated what she did to Luke and Matthew.

He assured me in the beginning that he would turn me into a ball of babbling flesh, and he did. For the majority of that morning after he was gone, I sat on my bed rolled into an emotional ball. I stared at the walls wondering just how – and if – we would ever completely recover. I didn't necessarily agree with the way I felt, but I felt that way nonetheless. Luke's sexual hang-ups began to make sense. His misaligned desires, the demands he barked while he choked me, even his fear of being in a relationship – it all became crystal clear. I felt helpless because I couldn't fix everything.

Frantically, I went through the house cleaning. Somehow convinced cleaning my home would clean up the mess, I scrubbed every inch of it until it was as sanitary as a hospital. I vacuumed the carpets until all of the lines from the vacuum's path were perfectly aligned. Then, I scrubbed the floors until the entire house smelled like Pine-sol. The sinks, the shower, the tub, the crumbs underneath the couch cushions. All spotless.

Like a woman possessed by cleaning demons I frantically searched for any remaining imperfections. I felt something was still out of place.

And I realized it wasn't my home that was dirty.

It was me.

I felt dirty, and it was the kind of dirty that couldn't be washed away. The memories of my friendship with Luke as a child had always been carefree and innocent. We held hands, swung in swings, and chased each other along the beach. As adults we continued all of those things.

We never stopped acting like we did when we were kids.

A week prior I believed two innocent childhood friends who lived innocent lives developed into two innocent adults who had similar sexual tastes. The sex was kinky, wild, and on the cusp of violent, but because the desires were derived innocently, I was convinced there was nothing wrong with us or the sexual acts.

After learning what happened to Luke, I no longer felt that we were innocent. I felt like the sex was a product of his mother's sexual abuse.

I wanted to find his mother. I wanted to find her and hurt her as much as she hurt my Luke. I felt a need to tell her that I knew what she had done, and that she was an evil woman who would be dealt with on judgement day.

But I didn't.

Instead, I prayed. I prayed for Luke to find a way to forgive her and for me to accept that I couldn't change a thing.

CHAPTER TWENTY-ONE

LUKE

"If you eat them one at a time they won't make you fat."

"They won't?"

He shook his head and grinned. "That's what abuela said. She said 'tell the surfer to don't fear the tamale.'"

I laughed. "Don't fear the tamale, huh? Well, tell her I'm not scared."

Juan was well aware I was conscious of what I ate, and that I chose to avoid foods that may made me feel overweight or unhealthy. For whatever reason, his grandmother decided to send a dozen tamales with him as a gift for me. Contrary to what I suspected his beliefs were regarding his offering, I accepted the package eager to find time to enjoy his grandmother's cooking.

I nodded my head in appreciation. "Have you tried them?"

He grinned. "They're pork and Anaheim chilies. They're my abuela's specialty and they're my favorite."

"You be sure to tell her I said thank you. And tell her if they're her specialty, I don't give a fuck if they're going to make me fat."

"I'll tell her, but I won't say the 'F' word. She'd smack me so hard my grandkids will feel it. That's what she tells me," he said with a laugh as he swatted his hand through the air.

I walked to the refrigerator, placed the tamales inside, and grabbed a bottle of orange soda.

I sat down on the bench and set the bottle of soda down beside me. "Have a seat."

He sat on the opposite end of the bench. "I've never seen you drink one of the bottles of pop. Not one."

"I don't drink soda."

"But you always have them in the cooler."

I had them there for one reason and one reason only. Juan liked them.

"They're for my guests."

He grinned and nodded as he opened the bottle on the end of the bench.

"So, I've been thinking," I said.

He took a drink of the soda, glanced in my direction, and waited for me to continue.

"You're a pretty good artist," I said.

He raised one eyebrow slightly. "According to who?"

"Well, when you were tagging all the buildings along the boardwalk, it was pretty apparent."

"Oh." He chuckled. "Yeah, I like to draw and stuff."

"Have you ever seen an airbrush?"

He nodded. "My uncle in Oceanside uses 'em. He paints motorcycles."

"You ever use one?"

He shook his head as he lifted the bottle of soda to his lips.

"You interested in learning?"

His eyes widened. "You gonna teach me?"

"Well, here's what I was thinking," I said. "About half of the boards I make have custom paint on them. It takes me as much time to paint them as it does to make them. So, I could make twice as many in the same amount of time if I didn't have to paint the fuckers."

He pursed his lips and gazed beyond me as if thinking. "Makes sense."

"I'll teach you how to use the airbrush. I don't think it'll take long. Then, once you've learned, I'll pay you to paint them."

His eyes widened slightly. He tipped the bottle of soda up and took another drink.

"I'll give you $200 a board. How's that sound?" I asked.

He jumped from the bench, coughed, and choked on the soda. Pinching his nose between his thumb and forefinger, he nodded eagerly.

"Sounds good," he responded in a nasal tone.

"You okay?"

He released his nose and nodded eagerly. "Swallowed wrong."

I stood. "So, that sounds fair. $200 for each board?"

He wiped the back of his hand against his nose. "Yes, Sir. So, when do you think you might be able to teach me?"

"Well, right now is good for me. So whenever works for you, we'll just make time to do it."

"Right now is good." His eyes fell to the floor. "Well, after I mop the pop up off the floor."

During the period of time that I had the shop, I never made a board in advance or in anticipation of a customer's desire or need. Instead, I chose to make them as customer's placed their orders, not necessarily needing the money or even caring much to provide the service.

In less than an hour, Juan had mastered the airbrushing technique, and was proving to be a natural at painting beach scenes.

I pulled my mask from my mouth and rested it on my chin. "I'm thinking we should have a few boards on display. You know, for sale."

He pulled his mask down and furrowed his brow. "We?"

"Well," I said. "If I'm making 'em, and you're painting 'em, what does that make us? Hell, we're damned near partners."

As the pride filled him he straightened his stance slightly. "Can I watch you? When you make them?"

"Sure," I said. "I'm not ready to give that part of it up. At least not yet. But you just as well learn."

He grinned and pulled his mask over his mouth.

"One more thing," I said.

He turned toward me and raised his eyebrows.

"No more Mr. Eagan. From here on out, I'm Luke," I said.

He pulled the mask down just long enough to respond. "Okay, Luke."

On that afternoon, Juan painted every piece of cardboard I had in the shop. By the end of the day the paint booth was filled murals of palm trees, sunsets, and beaches. One particular painting – a surfer riding the most perfect shaped wave – stood as a testament of Juan's ability to imagine and to convey his imagination accurately with paint.

We later shared a late lunch of tamales, and then he went home to tell his family the good news. I stuck around for a few more hours and fabricated a wooden frame for the picture of the surfer.

I hung the picture on the wall, stood back, and imagined the small speck of a man on top of the wave was me.

And for that short moment, my life was picture perfect.

CHAPTER TWENTY-TWO

LIV

"That was sure nice of you," I said.

He shrugged. "It gives me a little more time to do whatever. And, if I have a few boards in the shop for sale, whenever someone shows up, I won't feel like they're interfering with my schedule. I think it's an all-around good deal."

Luke's decision to let Juan paint the surfboards was obviously a way for him to deal with his feelings. I didn't know for sure, but I couldn't help but wonder if he had repressed the memories of what his mother did – only to remember them after she showed up at the hospital.

Either way, he seemed to be almost unaffected by the tragedy. I, on the other hand, was nothing short of obsessed with it. I guessed he had a lifetime to accept it, and I had only two days. Nonetheless, I was consumed by it completely.

When I looked at him I no longer saw my Luke. The man I had been in love with since childhood was gone. In his place a little boy whose innocence had been lost. A man with sexual desires developed at the hand of a sickening monster. He had become a childhood friend. A dinner companion. An associate.

I didn't want to touch him, and at least for the time being, I didn't want him to touch me. I wanted to go to sleep, wake up, and have it all be a dream.

As sickening as it made me feel to harbor the feelings, I couldn't change how I felt. I didn't blame him for anything that happened – and I accepted that he was the true victim – but it didn't seem to matter. Somehow I was convinced his mother's actions had developed his odd sexual appetite, and I felt my acceptance of his desires was in turn accepting his mother's behavior. Nothing was further from the truth. I had evolved from wanting to hurt her to wanting to kill her, and I wasn't a violent person.

I tried my best to act as if nothing between us had changed, but I doubted I was very convincing.

I forced a grin. "It sounds like a great plan."

He lowered his fork, peered over the table, and sighed. "Are you okay?"

"I'm fine." I nodded. "Just tired. I've been feeling sick."

"Hopefully you're not getting that shit that's going around."

"Hope not."

"So, Matt's going to go stay at dad's when they let him out. Kind of goes without saying, but he's going to be in a wheelchair for a while."

I continued to stare down at my plate. "That's good."

"You sure you're okay?"

I nodded, glancing up this time when I did. "I just don't feel good."

When we made eye contact, I smiled. I felt I had to. It seemed strange, but I didn't want to look at him. At least at that particular moment, he didn't interest me in the least. He was broken, and I felt I wasn't. My sexual appetite was developed because someone dropped me on my head, or maybe my mother ate too much raw fish while she was pregnant. Maybe my diaper wasn't changed often enough, who knows?

But I wasn't submissive because my father made me fondle his dick, or because my uncle played with my teenage twat. I was just the way I was because that's the way things were.

I wanted to hold Luke and provide him comfort – because I loved him. But at that moment I didn't feel that I loved him in a romantic sense. It was more of a feeling of obligation as his friend than anything else.

"Maybe we should just eat and go to bed," he said.

"I think it would be a good idea if you stayed at your place tonight. "I'd hate to get you sick," I said.

"If that's what you want," he said.

"It's not what I *want*, but I think it'd be best."

He finished his food, rinsed his plate, and placed it in the dishwasher. I continued to pick at my plate, hoping he would just leave. I felt like crying, screaming, and punching him in the chest all at the same time.

I felt confused, angry, lied to, cheated, and deceived. I rearranged the pieces of avocado in my salad trying to make myself believe that nothing was his fault, and that he was the same person regardless of what happened to him as a child, but nothing seemed to work.

As I became frustrated and pushed my salad to the side, his voice startled me slightly.

"I guess I'll go ahead and go."

"Okay," I said over my shoulder.

I heard the door close behind him, and instead of feeling sad or lonely, I felt relieved.

After I dumped my half-eaten plate of food into the trash, I walked into the bathroom and looked in the mirror. The skin underneath my eyes was black from lack of sleep. I didn't have on any makeup. I realized the clothes I was wearing were the same clothes I wore the day before. I stood and stared at myself wondering if I even remembered to take a shower.

My hair was flat.

I looked like death.

Everything inside of me was coming unraveled, and I knew it.

I realized I needed to address everything, and I knew the sooner I did so, the better I would feel about it. Instead of addressing it, I walked into my bedroom, climbed into bed, and went to sleep.

When my entire night's sleep was repeatedly interrupted by nightmares, I knew something needed to change.

And the thought of it made me sick.

CHAPTER TWENTY-THREE

LUKE

Point Loma was located due west of San Diego, where the land literally fell off into the depth of the ocean below. A great location to meditate, and as beautiful of a piece of land as God ever offered the inhabitants of the earth to enjoy, it was a place I frequented when I needed time to think.

Long before we began having sex I knew how I felt about her and chose not to act on my feelings for fear of losing her. I had spent a lifetime preserving something I held sacred, knowing no one or nothing could ever replace her. Now, it all seemed to be for not.

Liv seemed different after we spoke about my mother, and I felt foolish for telling her what happened. She didn't have to tell me how she felt, I could see it in her eyes. I had no idea if she was receding temporarily, or if something within her changed permanently. Either way I didn't like what I was seeing.

I sat on the edge of the cliff and watched the waves crash into the formation of rock below. Each and every one, be them slight or fierce, made an impact on the structural integrity of the earth beneath me. Over time, change would take place. Caverns would form, land would wash away, and more tide pools would develop.

Small causes having a large effect.

The butterfly effect.

In theory, something as small as a butterfly flapping its wings in Argentina may cause a tornado to develop in Oklahoma. The butterfly doesn't create the tornado, but the flapping of the wings at a particular time during certain weather conditions causes a change to the condition itself. Had the butterfly chosen to be still at that exact moment would the same thing have happened?

I stared into the tide pool and wondered. A small fish darted from beneath one rock to another. My mind drifted to another scenario.

Dropping a rock into the ocean creates ripples that cause the path of a swimming fish to be altered. Scheduled by nature to become a meal for a larger predator of the sea, the fish swims along a different path as a result of one ripple in the water. An alternate life begins, and over time the fish previously destined to die develops into the predator himself.

Because a pebble was dropped into the ocean.

My mother's actions changed me. I chose to reveal my mother's behavior to Liv, and in the end, my deepest fear seemed to be turning into reality.

Change, it seemed, was as inevitable as the tide.

CHAPTER TWENTY-FOUR

LIV

I finally decided that I felt uncomfortable. I wasn't angry or embarrassed, I was simply uncomfortable with what happened to Luke. Convinced his childhood abuse created the sexual drive within him, I felt if I participated in the act of having sex with him that I was indirectly condoning what had happened.

I hated myself for feeling the way I felt, but further felt if I didn't make some changes and make them quickly, that in addition to losing Luke as a lover, I may lose him as a friend.

The thought of losing him altogether was incomprehensible.

I wished I could turn back the clock to a time where none of what seemed to consume me even existed.

The distinct voice coming from the corner office made the hair on the back of my neck stand up. "Olivia, come here for a moment, please. Do you mind?"

I paused, turned around, and sighed lightly. Out of the view of the doorway leading into his office, I asked a question – even though I knew the answer. "Were you talking to me?"

"I was."

Shit.

I brushed the lint from my pants as I walked toward his office. After tugging the wrinkles from my shirt, I stepped through the door and peered over his massive desk.

"Yes?"

"You realize if there's something you need to talk about, you can always come to me, right?" he asked.

Mr. Davidson was in his late fifties, and an attractive man with neatly cropped salt and pepper hair. He reminded me of my father, and always treated his employees with respect, which was something I admired about him. It was disheartening to think that he was able to see what I believed I was hiding all so well. Luke always said he could see right through me and apparently Mr. Davidson could as well.

I forced a shitty little smile, glanced at the handful of papers I was holding, and tried to act preoccupied. "Uh huh. I'm okay."

"No, you're not," he said. "And you haven't been for some time."

I continued to adjust the stack of samples, acting as if it was more important than anything else at the moment. I wished he would give up and allow me to go back to my office and sulk, but expected he wasn't done with me yet. As he cleared his throat, I shifted my eyes up from the product samples.

"I'm fully aware your parents are in the middle of nowhere, so again, if you need to talk, I'm always here to lend an ear. Remember that, okay?" he asked.

I felt like crying. I nodded. My eyes quickly fell to the floor. "Thank you."

"Do you need some time off?" he asked.

"No, really. I'm fine. I just need to get this done by Friday, that's all," I said dryly.

"I tell you what. Friday's only two days away. After you get that done, why don't you take some time off? All you do is work, and you never take time for yourself. Take next week off, and don't even worry about using your vacation time. You and Luke just go to the beach or spend some time doing whatever you two enjoy, how's that?"

"His brother was hit by a car," I blurted.

I had no idea where the words even came from, they simply escaped my mouth like a sickness. As his eyes filled with concern, I continued.

"His legs are crushed, his arms are broken, and I don't know how to fix it," I babbled.

I began to softly cry.

I placed the paperwork I was clutching on the edge of his desk and wiped my eyes as he walked past me. He closed the door, walked to the edge of the desk, and opened his arms. I all but fell into him and allowed him to comfort me while I cried. None of the tears I shed were for Matthew, even though a few should have been.

They were all for Luke – and for me – because I had no idea how I was going to fix what seemed to wedge its way between us.

"Where is he?" he asked.

"At the beach." I leaned away from him and shook my head. "Oh, sorry. I mean Balboa."

"Flowers won't fix anything, but I'll have some sent, nonetheless. I'm so sorry. Why don't you leave your project with me and take the rest of the week off?"

I pulled away and wiped my eyes with my forearm, feeling foolish for having cried in the first place. "No, I'm just emotional. I'm sorry, I really don't have anyone to talk to about it."

I realized after I spoke that my statement made Luke look like a shit hat, and he wasn't any such thing. As much as I couldn't seem to bring myself to love him at the moment, I sure couldn't allow myself to hate him either.

"Well," I said as I collected my composure. "Except for Luke. It's just hard on him too."

He pushed his hands into the front pockets of his pants and nodded. "I'm sure it is. I'm so sorry. If I may ask, what happened?"

"He was. He was on his bicycle. A car drove off the road onto the bike path and hit him," I said softly.

He shook his head. "How tragic. Again, I'm so sorry. You can leave that file with me."

"No," I said, reaching for the file. "I just needed a good cry. I'm okay now."

"Very well," he said. "But I don't want to see you in here next week."

I clutched the file tightly and grinned. "Okay."

"Again, if you need anything," he said.

"I will," I responded, fully knowing I wouldn't.

I went back to my office, attempted to focus on my work, and found that I couldn't. After an hour of struggling to concentrate and being unsuccessful at doing so, I picked up my phone. For some time, I simply stared at the screen, hoping I could remain in limbo until everything was fixed. Eventually I decided I couldn't continue to treat Luke in the same manner, and I did what I knew I needed to do.

I typed him a text message.

I gazed down at what I had said.

We need to have a talk

Knowing I had full knowledge of what the talk would consist of – and that Luke had no earthly idea – my eyes welled with tears.

And I pressed send.

CHAPTER TWENTY-FIVE

LUKE

"You just have to be true to who you are, and if she's attracted to *that* person, you're golden," I said.

"Don't be a phony, right?" Juan asked.

I nodded. "You've got it."

"And that's all it takes?"

"It's not *all* it takes, but it's the first thing you need to be concerned with," I said. "Look at it this way. If you're trying to be someone you're not, whether it's to impress her or because you think it's what she wants, then she isn't falling for you, she's falling for whoever it is you're *trying* to be."

He shoved his hands into his pockets and shifted back and forth on the balls of his feet.

I raised my index finger in the air. "And sooner or later, because you're trying to be someone you're not, the real you will shine through. But *you* aren't who she fell in love with. She fell for the guy you were trying to be."

"I'm always me, it's just sometimes I do dumb stuff."

I lifted my chin slightly. "Like what?"

"I don't know. Like singing in the hallways and making up rap songs. You know, just dumb stuff."

"Has she heard you sing your rap songs?"

He chuckled. "*Everybody* has."

"And she likes you anyway?"

"She says she does."

"Then she likes *you*. That's the best start you can ask for," I said. "Just remember, always be true to you."

"I'm just nervous to go back. I can't wait to see her, though," he said.

"How much longer?" I asked.

"First day of school is September 8th."

"Well, you've got a month to prepare. You haven't seen her at all this summer?"

He shook his head. "No, she goes to Chula Vista to be with her dad for the summer."

I folded my arms in front of my chest and gave a half-hearted shrug. "Being away from someone you're affectionate toward sucks."

"What do you know about that?" he asked. "You see Liv every day. Ever since I been knowing you."

"I loved her for a long time before we got together. Let's just say not all of it was easy," I said. "I was away from her on an off, mentally at least."

He grinned. "I gotcha."

The front door opening caught my attention. After peering outside the paint booth and seeing someone in the shop, I tossed my head toward the front door. "Someone's here."

He looked like he was lost. Dressed in khaki-colored slacks, a silk short-sleeved button-down short, and huarache sandals, he gazed around the shop like he'd never seen a surfboard before. His tan looked like it was developed in a salon, and damned sure not earned from being in the sun.

"What can I help you with?"

"The one and only Luke Eagan." He said as he extended his hand. "I'm Peter Brisk with A.S.P. Have you got as few minutes?"

I shook his hand. "I've got the rest of my life, what can I help you with?"

His eyes shifted toward Juan. "You want to talk right here?"

"Haven't got anywhere else to go, so yeah. Oh, and this is Juan Ramirez. Juan, this is Peter Brisk."

"Nice to meet you, Sir," Juan said as he shook his hand.

"So, what can I help you with?"

"I'm going to cut right to it. A year or so ago, you were at Black's Beach. News 8 did a piece on you. We don't really know how that slipped past us, but it did. Anyway. We've done a little research on our end, and there's considerable interest in you. So, we'd like to make you an offer."

I studied his attire and his heavily greased hair. I fought not to laugh. "An offer for what?"

"Sponsorship," he said.

"You must have done too much research," I said sarcastically. "I don't surf pro."

He coughed a laugh and nodded eagerly. "We're well aware. We'd like for you to consider changing that, but if you don't, there's still interest."

"You want to sponsor me?"

He grinned and spread his arms wide. "We want to *represent* you. We're an agency of sports agents and professional marketers. We have a long list of people who want to sponsor you."

I had almost zero interest in listening to what he said, but decided to entertain him anyway. "Like who?"

"Red Bull, Oakley, Hurley, Billabong, Vans." He widened his eyes. "I could go on."

I shook my head. "Impressive, but there's no need."

"So, what are your thoughts? Do you have time to sit down and talk over your options?"

"Sorry, I'm really interested."

"When you hear how much money I'm talking about I think you'll change your mind. Luke, we're talking about seven figures over a three-year period," he said.

He raised his hands even with his chest and acted like he was holding something. "Seven. Figures."

I scoffed. "Sounds like a lot of money. But, I'm not for sale."

He smiled until he revealed all of his snow-white teeth. "Nobody wants to buy you, Luke. They only want a sticker on your surfboard and their name on your wetsuit."

"Appreciate it, but like I said."

"Let me leave a card with you." He reached into his pocket and pulled out a business card. "Here you go. Think about it, and give me a call when you get time."

I accepted the card and nodded. "Again, I appreciate it."

"Well." He glanced around the shop. "I'll be in touch."

He walked out of the shop and got into a new Mercedes-Benz. I turned to face Juan and wagged my eyebrows.

His eyes were as wide as saucers. "A million. That's seven figures."

I tossed the business card at him. "Sure is."

It fluttered to the floor at his feet. He bent down and picked it up. "And you don't care?"

I shrugged. "I'm flattered. But. Not interested."

"Staying true to yourself?"

I wagged my finger in the air. "You learn quick, Kid."

"No matter what it costs?" he asked.

"When you truly believe in something, money doesn't come into play," I said "Can *you* be bought?"

He shoved the business card into his pants pocket. "What do you mean?"

I turned my palm up and waved my hand in his direction. "Do you believe in God?"

"I'm Catholic," he said with a laugh. "So, yeah."

"If I was willing to give you a million bucks, but you had to stop believing in God and start worshiping the devil, would you?"

"No way," he snapped back.

I acted shocked. "Why?"

He puffed his chest slightly and rolled his shoulders back. "The devil isn't *my* God."

"Because that's your *belief*, right?"

He nodded. "It sure is."

"Well, that's my point. When you truly believe in something, nothing will change your mind. Not money, pressure from your peers, persuasive tactics." I waved my hands toward the door and laughed. "Not a new Mercedes-Benz."

"Nothing."

He grinned. "I like how you explain things. I'm glad we're friends."

"So am I," I said. "And I like how you're willing to listen."

"You going to tell Liv about turning that guy down?"

I glanced toward the bench. My phone was sitting at the end of it, where it had been all day. "I sure am."

I picked it up, swiped my thumb over the screen, and immediately realized I had missed a text message from Liv. After opening it, my heart sank.

"Everything okay?" Juan asked.

My concern must have been plastered all over my face.

"Yeah, everything's just fine," I lied.

But it wasn't.

A butterfly had just flapped its wings in Argentina.

And now I was forced to walk head-on into the eye of what I was certain to be terrible storm.

CHAPTER TWENTY-SIX

LIV

With my knees pressed together and my hands nervously sliding up and down the length of my thighs, I sat on the far end of the couch and drew a long breath. Even though I knew we needed to talk about how I felt, I didn't want to say anything. I still wanted everything that was bad to just go away, leaving Luke and me the way things were before.

I gazed down at the carpet. Seeing his expressions as I said what I had to say would only make matter worse.

I chewed against the inside of my lip. "We're going to need to stop having sex," I murmured.

"What? Why? What's going on, Liv?"

I glanced toward him, and upon seeing the concern in his eyes, I quickly shifted my gaze toward the carpet in front of me. "It isn't working out."

He coughed. "It isn't working out? What the fuck does that mean? It isn't *working out* because it just stopped. We haven't had sex since Matt was in the accident. It's been two weeks. Liv."

"I just can't keep doing it," I said. "I need to…I mean I want to…"

"You want to what?"

"I want to make sure we're still friends."

I shifted my eyes to Luke. His eyes had thinned to slits, and he was glaring back at me. My stomach quickly became filled with knots.

He clenched his fists and tucked them under his biceps. "I fucking swear. So, what happened? What changed?"

As far as I was concerned, I had no other option but to do what I was doing. If I attempted to continue a sexual relationship with Luke, I had no doubt we would be torn apart for good – I found the thought of sex with him repulsive. Ending our relationship while maintaining our friendship was the only way I could see us continuing.

And we had to continue.

Losing Luke altogether would crush me.

"I said *what changed*?"

I realized I had yet to answer him. I shrugged. "I don't know."

He offered a simple – but impossible – solution. "We can fix it."

It couldn't be fixed, and I was the only one who realized it. My eyes began to well with tears. "We can't."

"Can't or won't?" he growled.

I chewed on my lip and tried to slow the tears.

He jumped from the couch. "So, you're done? Just like that? I've got no say? Fuck, Liv. You haven't even told me why. I can't…"

He stepped directly in front of where I was sitting. I stared at his feet, afraid to look into his eyes.

"I can't live without you," he said.

I wiped my cheek with the back of my hand. I loved him more than anything, but I couldn't change how knowing what his mother did made me feel about having sex with him. I sat trying to convince myself that I wasn't the bad person – his mother was.

"I can't fucking do it. I love you, Liv. We need to fix this," he pleaded.

I glanced up. "I love. I love you, too."

His eyes filled with hope. Slowly, they widened.

"But I can't fix it," I said. "We just have to stop."

He lowered his head, ran his fingers through his hair, and raised his gaze to meet mine. The hope in his eyes was gone. He looked defeated.

"I'm not even going to try and explain how you make me feel," he said. "But I'll tell you this."

I swallowed heavily and stared.

"Now that I've had you, I'll never stop wanting you. And I've loved you for as long as I can remember. Fuck, Liv. It's all I fucking know."

His jaw muscles tightened. "I'll never stop loving you. I can't. But if you say we can only be friends, I'll agree. You know why?"

"Do you know why?" he asked, his voice stern and harsh.

My mouth was too dry to speak. It felt like someone had cut my chest open and removed my heart. I ached. My lips parted. I pressed my tongue to the roof of my mouth and attempted to swallow.

"Yes." I murmured.

"Because I can live without the sex. But I can't live without you."

And he turned and walked away.

CHAPTER TWENTY-SEVEN

LUKE

Although I didn't know for sure what caused Liv to want to end our relationship, I initially believed it had to have something to do with my sexual desires. However, after sitting on the beach and listening to the waves wash ashore for half the night, I wondered if her learning she was submissive opened an interest within her I wasn't completely capable of filling. I wasn't a Dom or a Master, nor did I want to be. I was just some guy who had strange sexual desires.

Regardless, ending our sexual relationship was what she wanted, therefore I felt compelled to give it to her.

When I was a teenager and began to spend the majority of my time surfing, I wanted my brother to surf with me. I felt the time spent together would allow us to bond, and hoped it would also serve as a means of us escaping from the lingering thoughts of our mother's abuse.

But Matt wasn't interested. Not in the very least. I complained to my father, and his response stuck with me throughout my adult life.

"Matt won't surf, he only wants to ride his stupid bike," I complained.

Working on the engine of his old Volkswagen Beetle, he motioned toward the side of the garage.

"Prop your board against the wall," he said.

I carefully leaned my board against the wall and walked back to the car. He wiped his hands on a rag and sighed.

"People are like animals, Luke," he said. "Naturally, all animals fit somewhere, and they fit well."

So far, what he said made had perfect sense, so I nodded my head.

"But when we try to make them fit in a place where they don't naturally belong, sooner or later, they'll resist. It isn't always at first, but eventually they will. Dogs will try and dig their way out of the yard, cats will sneak out of the house and hunt birds, and those snakes and lizards you and your brother catch? They always seem to get out of the aquarium. It's because we've got them in a place where they don't naturally belong."

"Like the big Lion at the zoo that's always asleep," I said. "You can tell he's pissed about being in there."

He nodded. "Just like the lion at the zoo."

"So, where we naturally belong." He placed his hand on my shoulder. "You like to surf. You're drawn to the water. Your brother likes to ride his bike, he's drawn to the land. You'll never convince him to be a surfer, and he'll never convert you into a cyclist. Because it's not where you naturally belong."

"But surfing is fun. And it's relaxing," I explained.

"As far as *you're* concerned," he said. "Listen, Luke. Never try to force a rattlesnake to climb a tree. It'll only piss off the rattlesnake and eventually get you bit. Don't forget that."

And I never forgot.

Apparently, from a sexual standpoint, Liv didn't belong with me. For me to try and force her to accept my desires as being her own was no different than trying to force a rattlesnake to climb a tree.

I stood, brushed the sand from my legs, and stretched. I didn't need to try and convince Liv to be with me. I needed to accept that in time she would naturally end up where she belonged. All I could do was pray that with whoever or wherever she settled pleased her.

Because seeing her cry created a pain within me that I was afraid time may never heal.

CHAPTER TWENTY-EIGHT

LIV

In 48 hours I had experienced every feeling imaginable. Currently, I was in a state of depression. Now with nine consecutive days that I wasn't expected to be at work, I had my doubts that I would be able to get through it without having to admit myself into the hospital for mental reasons.

Realizing I had to let Luke go to save our friendship and accepting that we would never be in a relationship were two totally different things. I had no doubt what I had chosen to do was the right thing, and I fully realized doing so would potentially save our friendship. Accepting that we would never again be romantically involved, however, seemed to be impossible.

I had been in bed since 7:00 on the previous night, and it now was past noon – but I could find no way to get up.

My heart hurt.

With Luke, I felt like I could be myself, which was something I never felt with another man. He accepted me for who I was, and in doing so, he made me feel that it was okay to simply be me.

When Luke walked into the room, I felt energized, which always seemed to immediately be followed by feelings of exhaustion. In his presence, my mind sped along at ten times the pace of normal, thinking of what we might do together before he left. Often, I would find myself anticipating the next time he would touch me, only to later see that an hour had passed without me doing so much as moving from my place on the couch.

When he did touch me it was magical. Tracing his fingertip along the edge of my jaw would send me into a frenzy, but I never shared with him the effect his touch had on me. For him to realize how powerful a simple touch of his hand could be might have caused him to do so more frequently – and in turn change the intensity I felt when he did.

A risk I wasn't willing to take.

And now, accepting that I would never receive his affectionate touch again caused excruciating pain deep within my being – I felt as if my soul was being torn out. The less I accepted it, the more pain I felt. The closer I came to accepting it, the more my soul felt as if it were being ripped from my chest.

Luke was the perfect friend, the perfect man, the perfect gentleman, and the perfect lover.

I stared at the ceiling, incapable of doing much more, wishing I could simply scoop out the part of my brain that took exception to him being molested by his mother. My inability to accept it as being something out of his control caused me to feel shallow and malevolent.

I rolled over, buried my head in the pillow, and allowed my mind to drift to thoughts of moving to St. Louis. The thought of abandoning the ocean, which once seemed incomprehensible, now appeared to be the only answer to my problem.

A few minutes later, the thought of leaving Luke seemed realistic.

My stomach convulsed. I coughed.

I ran to the bathroom.

And I vomited.

Attempting to accept leaving Luke had actually made me ill.

But the thought of living in his presence – and without his love – was slowly crushing me.

CHAPTER TWENTY-NINE

LUKE

I raised my clenched fist, hesitated, and sighed heavily. It wasn't a forced sigh seeking attention or to make a point, it naturally escaped my lungs as an expression of relief. There was always something comforting about going home.

It seemed strange knocking, but I had no alternative. I tapped my knuckles against the door three times and waited.

The garage door was up, and the Volkswagen was sitting in the garage beside his Chevy Truck. As I stood in wait, I craned my neck at the sight and grinned. It seemed no different than when I was a kid. The vehicles and the garage were spotless. As far as my father was concerned there was a place for everything and everything was to be in its place.

I turned toward the house as I heard the bolt slide to unlock the door.

Dressed in faded blue shorts, and an even more faded surf tank, he looked the same as he always did. He pulled the door open and stood to the side. "I always figured there'd be a formal announcement – or something on the news at least. I can't believe it happened without someone saying *something*."

I stepped inside the house. "About what?"

"Hell freezing over," he said, turning to walk into the house. "Apparently it's happened, but I didn't get the memo."

"I've been busy."

He glanced over his shoulder. "For seven years?"

I followed him into the house and didn't bother responding. He wasn't angry, and I knew it. He had his own way of dealing with his feelings, and joking about what bothered him was his manner of letting me know he was disappointed with me for my infrequent visits. It wasn't that I *never* paid him a visit, but each time I did was on a holiday – something he perceived as a requirement, not a choice.

"So who died?" he asked as he sat down in his chair.

"No one. Well, not really," I said.

"Is someone half-dead? Is it someone I know?"

I sat down across from him and struggled with what I wanted to say. As I situated myself on the couch and tried to get mentally comfortable, he reclined in his seat and tossed his hands into the air.

"Where's your sidekick?"

"Liv? She's at home."

"Not working today? She didn't lose her job, did she?"

I shook my head. "No, she's on vacation."

My father looked like he could have been my twin, if it was twenty years prior. As a kid, I always referred to him as a hippie, but as an adult, I didn't necessarily look at the *hippie* description as accurate. He had hair about as long as mine, and wore a beard more often than he didn't. Both of his ears were pierced, and he never took his earrings out – at least that I could remember. Tattoos covered both arms, and although he didn't surf very frequently when I was young, he had been doing it more often since Matt graduated high school.

"Should have brought her," he said. "She's more entertaining than you, and a damned sight easier on the eyes."

"That's why I'm here," I said.

"Liv?"

I nodded. "Yeah."

"She okay?"

"Just give me a minute. I'll try and explain everything, but I don't want to argue about this. And I don't really want to turn it into a joke, either. I'd like to have a serious talk."

"Whenever you're ready."

I rested my forearms on my thighs and clasped my hands together. "About three months ago, Liv and I started seeing each other. You know, sexually. Boyfriend-girlfriend. Whatever you want to call it."

He nodded. "Okay."

"Well, everything went great until the end of last week."

He lowered his head, raked his fingers through his hair, and lifted his gaze to meet mine. "What happened?"

"Well, that's the deal. I don't know. But let me tell you some other shit I *do* know, and then we can talk. Some of it's about your ex-wife, just so you're aware."

He lowered his chin slightly and kept his eyes locked on mine. One of the things I always admired about my father was that he always maintained eye contact when he spoke.

I stood, walked to the glass door that opened out onto the deck, and gazed through the glass. "So, with Valerie – and with Liv – the sex wasn't *normal*. I've always been a little weird about sex. Kinky or whatever. I think I knew all along what it was that caused it, but I never really admitted it. Not to myself or to anyone else. Well, now I can't help but see that I'm the way I am because of what happened."

I glanced in his direction for a moment, eventually turning toward the door again. "So, it ended up Liv was just like me as far as her sexual tastes went. Hell, we were both wondering what took us so long to get together. Then after Matt was in the hospital, things went to shit."

"Did she ever know? Liv?" he asked.

Still gazing through the glass, I shook my head. "Not until the other day. After the little outburst in the hospital, I had to tell her. And it was after that when things went to hell."

"So, you're wondering if that had something to do with it? Her finding out?"

I walked back to the couch and sat down. "No, I *know* it has something to do with it. I've had too much time to think about it. I just don't know how to fix it."

"Might not be able to fix it." He shook his head and stood. "Something to drink?"

"Water?"

"Got plenty of that. Anything else?"

"Unless you've got Liv in there, no."

"Can't help you there, Son."

A few minutes later, he returned with two bottles of water, tossing one into my lap without warning. I caught it inches before it landed in my crotch.

"Still have good reflexes," he said. "You still study?"

"Every winter. I don't surf as much in the winter, so I go from November to March."

He lowered himself into his chair. "Good for keeping your head screwed on straight."

"Well, it doesn't seem to be helping much," I said.

"So, back to what you were asking," he said. "Lemme think."

I opened my water and took a few sips, waiting for his words of wisdom. After adjusting himself in his chair and drinking half of his bottle of water, he met my gaze.

"Well, if you two were compatible before the run-in with your mother, and she broke it off with you after, there's no arguing that her finding out had something to do with it. My guess is either she was abused and it triggered something, or she just can't process what happened to you as something she can accept."

"I don't think she was abused." I said.

He cocked an eyebrow and waved the neck of his water bottle in my direction. "I doubt she thought you were, either."

"Good point."

"As far as the other thing goes? Hell, it's anyone's guess," he said.

"I agree."

He cocked his head to the side slightly and furrowed his brow. "So why exactly are you here, Son?"

"I want her back. I can't even force myself to think about trying to live without her."

"She isn't talking to you?"

"She is, but I mean I want her back as my girlfriend, my lover, whatever you want to call it."

"I see," he said.

He unscrewed the lid from the bottle of water, lifted it halfway to his mouth, and hesitated. "Well, here's my advice."

I leaned forward and fixed my eyes on his. He nonchalantly drank the remaining water, screwed the lid back on the bottle, and tossed it at me.

"Go talk to her," he said.

I stood up and tossed my hands in the air. "That's your advice?"

"What'd you expect? A pick up line?"

"I expected *something*."

"Well," he said as he fought to climb out of the reclined chair. "You got damned good advice and a $1.00 bottle of water. You taste that hint of lime?"

I lifted the bottle, looked at the label, and shook my head. "No."

"Me neither," he said. "But I pay extra for it. That's kind of what I'm saying. Sometimes you miss things in life because there's no contrast. I bet if I told you that water had a lime in it before you drank it you'd have tasted it."

"I don't get it."

"She's a woman, Son. They talk in circles and think they've explained themselves. If you don't understand why she's left you, you need to ask her, not me. And ask until you find out what it is you're after. You're not seeing what it is because it's faint. But I can damn sure guarantee you she's hinted at it. Just like that lime."

"You said there's no contrast. What did you mean?" I asked.

"Between you," he said. "You two are too much alike. There's no contrast. If she was different than you, whatever it was would stand out like a cock on a cake. But she's the same, so there's no contrast."

I grinned and nodded my head. "I'll go talk to her."

"Your brother's getting screws in his legs. Should be out in a week."

"I'll get up there and see him," I said.

"No you won't, but it's nice to hear you say it," he said.

He opened his arms. "Give your old man a hug."

I gave him a short hug, feeling the entire time that the talk did me some good. I realized I often thought about what my father said long after we stopped talking. I wasn't sure if it was that his advice was so well thought out, or if I simply admired him enough to give him far more credit than he was due. I raised the water bottle as I turned away. A *hint of lime*. I chuckled and turned toward the door.

I finished the bottle of lime water as I sauntered toward the door. It tasted like plain old water. As I reached for the door handle I said my parting remarks. "I'll let you know how things work out."

"See you Christmas," he responded.

The sad thing was that I knew he was right.

CHAPTER THIRTY

LIV

"I need you to promise me you won't say anything about what I'm going to tell you, ever," I said.

Chloe shook her head as she inhaled a deep breath. "I'll tell you what you *need*. You need to start trusting people. Whatever you and I talk about is between us, always. You make me feel like we're sixteen. And who in the fuck dressed you this morning? You look like shit."

Her hair was dirty blonde with pink highlights. Dressed in jean shorts, Chuck's, and a vintage *Ziggy Stardust and the Spiders from Mars* tee shirt, she looked cute. I, on the other hand, looked like I had just escaped a mental ward.

Wearing jeans, old combat boots from high school, and a light jacket over a tee shirt I had worn for the last four days, I could have passed for a homeless girl.

"I feel like shit, too," I said. "And I'm sorry. I do trust you."

"Then act like it."

"Okay."

I shoved my hands into the pockets of my jacket and fixed my eyes on the far corner of the table. After what seemed like an eternity of silence, I found the nerve to speak. "You said when we first met and talked about stuff that most people who are like we are just end up this way. You said there's not anything that makes us like this. That we weren't abused. You said we're normal. You said that."

She raised her hand between us. "Hold up. You're doing what you always do. You're twisting shit around, Liv. What I said was that nothing *had* to happen to make someone have the desires or characteristics of a submissive."

She cleared her throat and continued. "Statistically speaking, there's 'X' amount of people in this world who were mistreated as kids. So, statistically speaking, there's 'Y' amount of people who are submissive and have been mistreated as kids. I don't know what 'X' and "Y' are, but I know they're significant."

I glared at her. "How'd you know I was talking about being abused as kids?"

"What the fuck is wrong with you?" she snapped back. "You mentioned it, that's how."

I rubbed my eyes with the heels of my palms and tried to collect my thoughts. "I'm sorry, I haven't slept for a week."

She leaned against the edge of the table, narrowed her eyes, and stared. "You said this was an emergency. What the fuck is going on?"

After a few seconds of preparing my perfect response, my bottom lip began to quiver. "Luke and I broke up," I sobbed.

"Oh shit. I'm sorry. What happened?"

In response, I cried uncontrollably for some time – partially due to exhaustion, but more as a result of being completely heartbroken. After exhausting myself of tears, I took a choppy shallow breath and wiped my eyes on the arms of my jacket.

"I uhhm. I…"

"I found out."

"He was cheating?" she asked.

I shook my head. "No."

"When he was a kid. His uhhm. His mother abused him."

Keeping my response brief made saying it much easier than I expected. The abuse, as far as I was concerned, was ten times easier to accept than being without Luke. Speaking about it seemed to hold the same values.

She sat up straight. "I'm sorry. His parents divorced when we were in middle school, right?"

I nodded. "Yeah."

After what seemed like an extended period of awkwardly fidgeting in my seat, she broke the silence.

"So what happened between you two?"

"I found out about it, you know, about his mom. And I couldn't get over it," I said. "All I could think about was that his mom abusing him made him the way he was. And it creeped me out to think about having sex with him. Like, if I was having sex with him, I was condoning or approving his mother's behavior."

She stared back at me as if I had three heads. "What?"

I shrugged. "What?"

She glared at me for a moment, leaned against the back of her seat, and slowly shook her head. "Let me get this straight. You find out Luke was abused as a child and instead of supporting him, you broke up with him. You decided if you supported him that you're supporting his mother's abuse? So you fucking walked away?"

It sounded bad the way she worded it, but I nodded my head nonetheless.

Her eyes narrowed to slits. "What the fuck is wrong with you?"

A few seconds later, and the crying began again.

"I don't know," I blubbered. "It's just…his mom…his mom made him that way…it's just…"

"It's just what?" she snapped.

"Gross. It's gross," I cried.

"Really? The same guy you were bragging about a few months ago is gross now? Because his mother abused him?"

I nodded.

"You selfish *bitch*," she hissed.

I had called Chloe in an act of desperation, hoping for sympathy and advice. It didn't appear she was willing to give much of either. I was beginning to feel smaller and smaller.

"And I thought you went to school for graphic design."

I wiped the tears from my eyes. "I did."

"Oh," she said. "There for a minute I was thinking maybe you went to medical school and I didn't know about it."

I stared back at her, confused. "Huh?"

"You've diagnosed Luke. You've decided that his mother made him the way he is. What if she didn't? It's common medical knowledge that a small percentage of people in the lifestyle are abused. So who's to say his abuse caused his kink?" She crossed her arms in front of her chest. "You don't have a medical degree, so it's sure as fuck not you."

I wiped my nose with the back of my hand. "So you think maybe he was just born like that?"

She leaned forward slightly. "You're as dumb as a sack of sand."

As I prepared to respond, she turned her palm up and held it between us. "You're done thinking. *Done*. I'm doing the thinking for you from here on out."

I chewed the inside of my lip and nodded my head.

"Okay," she said. "You're just freaking out. He was abused. It's fucking sickening, especially when it's a mother doing it. We think of our mom as someone who will always nurture us. And when one of them does that? It's pretty hard to accept. I'm sure that's part of what's got you all fucked up. Personally, I'd like to tie his mom up and throw knives at her."

"But. That's no reason for you to abandon Luke. He needs your support, and you need to find a way to give it. Here's my idea." She extended her index finger. "You and Luke. Together. You confront her."

"What? Confront her? I can't do that," I responded.

"Sure you can," she said. "Confrontation is the quickest way for someone who was abused to start to recover. It allows the abused to feel empowered, finally be heard, and more than anything, it's cleansing."

I slumped in my seat and stared. "Says who?"

She cocked one eyebrow.

I covered my hand with my mouth.

She nodded. "You guessed it."

I lowered my hand. "Oh my God, I…"

"Save it." She chuckled. "I don't need you tossing my ass to the curb."

"So, Luke and me both? At the same time?" I asked.

"Yeah, if he'll agree to it. if you're both there, it'll make it much easier on each of you. This might sound crazy to you, but basically you grew up with him. His family was your family. His mom abusing him probably makes you feel like she let you down. Almost like she abused you."

What she was saying made perfect sense. As crazy as confronting

Luke's mother sounded, somehow as I considered it as being a viable solution, I began to fill with hope. Within a few minutes, I was convinced it just might work.

"I think it's a good idea," I said.

"It's a great idea," she said with a grin.

I pushed my cup of coffee to the side, realizing I hadn't so much as taken a drink. "Thank you."

"One more piece of advice?" she asked.

"Sure."

"Take a shower," she said. "And change clothes,"

I nodded my head and stood, eager to see if her idea would work.

She opened her arms. "If you do talk to her…"

Exhausted, I held her in my arms, appreciative to have her as a friend. "Yeah?"

"Be sure and let it all out. All the anger, all the feelings, everything. And tell Luke to make her apologize. If she will, it'll make a big difference."

"Okay," I said.

"Good luck," she said. "And let me know how it goes."

"I will."

As I released her I caught a whiff of myself. Chloe was right, I needed a shower. Maybe after a long bath, I thought, I would feel good enough to call Luke.

And I hoped he still loved me enough to answer.

CHAPTER THIRTY-ONE

LUKE

"I just need you to listen. Like, for maybe a few minutes without talking, okay?" Liv asked.

We had simultaneously sent each other text messages wanting to have a talk. After sitting on her porch waiting for her to get home for almost half of an hour, I was willing to listen to whatever she had to say.

"Okay," I said.

She looked like hammered shit, and smelled like she hadn't taken a bath in a week, but seeing her was comforting.

"So I'm going to be honest, like *really* honest. And it wasn't that I lied when we talked before, but I didn't tell you *everything*."

I nodded. "I'm just going to listen."

"Okay," she said as she rubbed her hands together frantically.

Apparently, she was pretty excited about whatever she had to say.

I studied her as she gazed down at the floor. There were dark circles under her eyes, her face had absolutely no makeup on it whatsoever, and her hair was a matted mess. She was wearing an old tee shirt I had left at her house when I was a senior in high school, and although it was the middle of summer, she was dressed in jeans and combat boots. Despite her odd outward appearance, as she sat and mentally prepared for whatever it was she intended to say, she was beautiful.

She took a long deep breath.

"So when I found out about your mom it freaked me out I convinced myself that her abuse made you crave the things you crave sexually and I felt like if I enjoyed participating in those same things it somehow made me a part of all the abuse or that I condoned it or something I don't know but the whole thing freaked me out and I didn't want to lose you as a friend and I knew if we kept having sex it would freak me out so I broke up with you but it drove me crazy and I've been crying for a week and I haven't slept or taken a bath in a week either but I talked to Chloe and she said if you and me together confronted your mother that it would be the first step in recovery and I really need you back so I was wondering if you'd consider that?" she blurted in one long breathless sentence.

I raised my index finger and inhaled a shallow breath. As I prepared to respond the best I felt I was able, she interrupted my thought process.

"Wait," she snapped. "I'm not done."

"Okay."

"So I want you and me to go talk to your mom. Will you do that?" She asked. "Okay, I'm done."

"Wow." I widened my eyes and shook my head.

"So you…" I paused and thought about everything she said, realizing I was speaking more out of excitement than preparedness.

"You want to confront my mother? About the abuse? You and me?" She nodded her head eagerly.

My eyes fell to her feet and slowly raised to meet her gaze. "It's something I've been wanting to do for a long time, but never thought I'd be able to without beating the shit out of her. If you'll go with me, I think it's a good idea."

She clapped her hands together. "I hope this works."

I chuckled. "But you'll need to take a shower and change clothes first."

She jumped from the couch. "I will. Get it set up. When do you think we can do it?"

I shrugged. "I'm guessing if we ask, it'll never happen. If this is what's between you and me being together, I say we just go to her office. Fuck it. She interfered with my life, I say it's time we interfere with hers."

"I'll be ready in fifteen minutes."

"Take your time."

As she took a shower, I thought of what I wanted to say. It seemed odd that Liv's resolution to our problem was the same resolution I had thought of for years, but never seemed to develop the courage to proceed with.

The more I thought about it, the more prepared I felt I became. I didn't want to be my mother's friend, her enemy, or her son, for that matter. As far as I was concerned, she forfeited her right to be my mother when she chose to do the things to me that she did.

I wanted to say what I felt I needed to, walk away, and hopefully live a less complicated life as a result.

One with Liv in it.

She stepped through her bedroom door and into the living room. She looked gorgeous. I wanted to get up, hold her in my arms, and give her a long passionate kiss. I wished things were the way they were before, but realized the healing process for both of us would take time.

"You look gorgeous," I said.

"Thank you." She tossed her hair. "Are you ready?"

I felt I'd never actually be ready.

It had been thirteen years.

Thirteen years of nightmares. Thirteen years of guilt. Thirteen years of feeling abandoned. Thirteen years of wanting answers. Thirteen years of wanting an apology. And, thirteen years of wanting closure.

"Yeah," I said. "I am."

It was time for me to get closure.

And to begin a new chapter in my life.

CHAPTER THIRTY-TWO

LIV

"I'm sorry, Eve isn't taking visitors at the moment, if you'd like to leave your name and telephone number, I'll see to it that she returns your call," the receptionist said.

"Where's her office," Luke demanded.

"I'm sorry, Sir. She's got a full schedule, and I'll really need you to…"

"Come on, Liv," Luke said as he reached for my hand.

"Sir, Ma'am...Sir…Sir…" she wailed as Luke began stomping down the long hallway, dragging me along with him.

It seemed like a great idea, but after we arrived, my stomach was doing flips. I felt there was no way I would be able to say everything I needed to if we actually got to talk to her, and I couldn't help but wonder if my hope of repairing everything was going to remain just that – hope.

Luke glanced through the door of each office he angrily made his way toward the end of the hallway. After being met by three wide-eyed men who apparently didn't want to argue, his mother stepped into the hallway.

"Come in," she said as she turned toward her office.

With my heart beating so fast it felt like I was going to pass out, I followed Luke into the office. He pushed the door closed and inhaled a deep breath. His mother, dressed in a black business suit, looked remarkably normal.

I guess I expected when we confronted her that there would be horns on the side of her head, even though I knew her to be an attractive woman. In my mind she had transformed into an evil monster, and regardless of how she appeared at that moment, she would always remain a demon.

"We're going to talk," Luke said. "And you're going to listen."

She sat down at her desk and gazed back at him with hollow eyes. She didn't gaze past him, or even attempt to look away, which shocked me. Her eyes, however, conveyed absolutely no emotion. I glanced at Luke.

"Go ahead," I said.

"I hate you for what you did to me. I'll never stop hating you, and as much as I want to forgive you, I can't. Don't ask me to," he said, shaking his finger in her direction as he spoke. "Ever."

With an emotionless face, she stared back at him. Hearing Luke speak seemed to make me more comfortable. As he continued, I stayed focused on her, and the more I studied her, the less threatening she appeared to be. She wasn't a demon or the devil, she was a coward.

"What you did? I thought it changed me forever. But it didn't, and I won't give you the fucking satisfaction of thinking you have that kind of power over me. You're a heartless bitch that will one day have to meet your maker knowing what you did to Matt and me was so far beyond wrong that they'll have to make a special place in hell for you to live in."

She blinked. A tear rolled down her cheek. I found it odd that she didn't even attempt to wipe it away. She simply sat and stared back at him as if she deserved to hear everything he was saying.

He turned toward me. "Liv?"

I inhaled a deep breath, gazed down at her desk, and raised my eyes to meet hers. The words came much easier than I thought, but in hindsight, it may have been that I desperately wanted to fix what was broken between Luke and me.

"When I found out what happened, I wanted you to die. Actually, I wanted to kill you. Now I don't want that. I want you to suffer instead. That's why I'm here. I want you to know what you did to Luke doesn't only affect him, it affects me. And I want you to know how wrong it is, and I want you to drown in it. I want you to choke on it. And I want every day of your life to be filled with regret."

Her lips parted.

"No!" I shouted. "I'm. Not. Done."

"You're supposed to love your kids. Protect, honor, support, and cherish them. You failed. You betrayed him. You are a nasty rotten bitch," I half-shouted. "And you're fucking sick."

I didn't need to go any further. I already knew what we had done somehow worked. I stood at the edge of her desk, shaking and filled with emotion, but I also stood knowing I loved Luke more than any other person on the earth.

"I guess that's my job now. To love him, honor him, support and cherish him. I can tell you what I won't do." I raised my index finger in the air. "Betray him. That'll *never* happen."

Her eyes shifted to Luke. Another tear rolled down her cheek.

And another.

"I want an apology," Luke said. "Not an explanation. An apology."

She cleared her throat. "Luke. I'm so sorry. I'm sorry for what I did, I truly am. I wish I could make it all go away, but I can't. There isn't a day that goes by that I don't regret…"

Luke raised his hand. "Stop. Save it. I've heard all I need to hear."

He turned to face me and sighed. "Anything else?"

I craned my neck toward her. I wasn't afraid. I knew she couldn't hurt me, and she was done hurting my Luke.

"I hate you," I fumed.

I thought the visit would be tiring, emotional, and exhausting. After telling her I hated her, I was full of energy and free of worry. But above all, I felt cleansed.

Luke cleared his throat, reached down, and gripped the edge of the desk in his hands. As her tear-filled gaze met his, he spoke. "I'll pray for the ability to forgive you, but I'll never forget what you did."

He turned to face me. "Ready?"

I held out my hand. He reached out and held my hand in his.

Together, hand-in-hand, we walked down the hall. Past the bitch receptionist, into the parking lot, and to my car.

I released his hand and fumbled in my purse for the keys.

"What now?" I asked.

He inhaled a deep breath, exhaled, and grinned. "Let's start over."

"What do you mean?"

"Ice cream. At Belmont Park. That's what we were doing when everything went to shit. Let's just forget any of this happened and start over."

"Ice cream? Seriously?"

As he reached for the door handle, his hair fell into his face. He hadn't shaved for a few days, and the beard I loved was returning. He raked his fingers through his hair and looked up. "Yeah. And maybe the rollercoaster again."

"I love you. And I'm sorry."

"Don't be." He grinned. "If it wasn't for you freaking out, this would have never happened. I can't even tell you how this made me feel."

"You don't have to," I said. "I know."

"Because there's no contrast," he said.

"Huh?"

He shook his head. "We'll talk about it some other time."

I smiled and opened the car door confident we'd have the rest of our lives to talk about it.

CHAPTER THIRTY-THREE

LUKE

I reached between her legs with my right hand as I fixed my eyes on hers. Her mouth opened slightly and her eyes widened as I slid my middle finger inside. She arched her back slightly and inhaled a shallow breath.

I added another finger.

She closed her eyes and chewed against her bottom lip.

Slowly, I began to slide my finger in and out of her. With each stroke, my fingers became more lubricated. After enough strokes to hear her breathing become slightly labored, I buried my fingers as deep as I could and curled the tips of them upward.

Her eyes opened.

"I want that dick."

"Shhh." I flipped my hair out of my eyes and grinned. "This is an experiment."

I curled my fingertips again, teasing her g-spot.

Her eyes fell closed.

I studied her as I continued to torture her. With my eyes remaining fixed on her face, I adjusted myself on the comforter and reached for her nipple with my free hand. She initially pulled away, only to exhale sharply and relax onto the bed beside me.

Twisting her nipple between my thumb and forefinger, I continued to work my fingers in and out of her now completely soaked pussy. With every other stroke, I curled the tips of my fingers into the sensitive spot directly above them.

She opened her eyes and raised herself onto her elbows. "I need it. I do."

I slid my fingers deep and held them in place.

Her back naturally arched. "No more experiments. Fuck me."

I grinned and shook my head.

"Let me suck your cock."

With my fingers buried deep inside of her, I curled them upward, dragging the tips along the inner wall of her tightness. As my fingers pressed against her g-spot she fought to get away, squirming toward the headboard of the bed.

"Fuck my mouth," she said.

"Hold still."

"I can't. I'm sorry. I need your cock. Let me see it."

I shook my head. She pulled away from me and sat up.

She pressed her hands against my shoulders. "You fucker."

Playfully, I let her push me onto my back. As I rolled over, my cock stood straight at attention, pointing directly at the ceiling.

"I'm riding that cock," she said as she climbed on top of me.

Although I hadn't shared my feelings with Liv, since our confrontation with my mother, my manhood seemed to have a mind of its own. Previously, my mind had to be filled with devious thoughts for me to be erect, and now all I had to do was see Liv.

The thought of a woman riding my cock had never appealed to me, and in fact, it had been tried a few times, all of which had been unsuccessful.

Anxious to see if it would work, I fought back very little.

"If you're going to ride it, you better *ride* it."

Facing me, she grinned and reached between her legs. She slid two of her fingers into herself and lifted her hand between us. "Look, soaked."

"I know."

She gripped my shaft in her hand, stroked it twice, and lifted her ass slightly from my thighs. As she lowered herself, moaning the entire time, her tight pussy enveloped the entire length of my cock.

"Watch," she groaned.

I cleared my throat. "Excuse me?"

"Watch!" she demanded, nodding her head toward my waist.

She wiggled her hips, grinding her wet pussy onto the base of my shaft. "No, better idea."

"Count."

I interlocked my fingers behind my head and stared up at her. "What?"

"Count," she commanded.

She lifted her weight from me until the lips of her pussy barely encompassed the head of my dick. Hovering above me on shaking legs, she peered down at me and grinned. "Say *one*."

"One," I said.

She released herself and thrust the entire shaft deep inside.

"I love your big cock," she moaned.

"I love your tight little pussy."

"When I lift up, you say how many strokes we're on," she said. "Ready?"

I grinned and nodded.

She lifted herself again.

I gazed down at my glistening cock. "Two."

She grinded herself down onto my hips. The feeling of her tight pussy squeezing my cock was almost more than I could handle. Having had always been in charge of what was happening in any of my sexual adventures, I found the excitement of not knowing very arousing.

I closed my eyes and allowed myself to become lost in the feeling.

Watch!" she barked.

I opened my eyes. With my throbbing shaft still buried deep inside of her, she reached up and squeezed her boobs in her hands, pinching her nipples between her thumbs and forefingers.

"You watching?"

I nodded eagerly.

She lifted her weight, slowly exposing each inch of my cock as it escaped her tight grip.

"Two. No. Three. Three!" I said as I saw the rim appear.

"Fuck it. You don't count worth a fuck." she said. "And I don't have the patience for this shit."

She began to work her hips back and forth rapidly, teasing my cock with precision. I closed my eyes as she continued, fearful that I might not make it for long. As she bucked her hips and forced my entire cock inside of her with each perfectly timed stroke, I closed my eyes and focused.

Her pussy was magical, fitting my girth perfectly. Tight enough that the first few strokes needed to be taken slowly and with great care, but forgiving enough to allow full penetration after a reasonable amount of foreplay.

"Fuck yes," she wailed. "I'm going to come all over you."

She continued to thrust her hips back and forth, tossing her head from side to side as she did. Her hair bounced about, falling down and partially covering her boobs, only to be tossed to the side with the next stroke.

As I felt her contract around my shaft, I held my breath.

"Fuck yes, fuck yes, fuuuuuck yes…" she moaned as she held the entire length deep inside of her.

I felt myself begin to swell.

Slowly, she lifted herself up the shaft.

After holding still for a short second, she shoved it deep again.

I arched my back, opened my eyes, and absorbed every ounce of her being.

And I burst inside of her.

She let out a moan of pleasure, and although she held still, her vaginal walls massaged my cock, milking it of every drop of cum.

"Fuck yes," she breathed as she collapsed on top of me.

I pushed up on her shoulders, lifted her from me, and gazed into her eyes. "You think you're done?"

"My twat is throbbing," she said.

"Fuck *my* mouth," I demanded.

"No contrast," she said.

I shook my head and stared. "Excuse me?"

She grinned. "Let's fuck *each other's* mouths."

There was no doubt about it. We were truly cut from the same cloth, and there was no contrast between us.

She rolled over, turned around, and lowered her pussy onto my face. As I shoved my tongue deep into her, she wrapped her wet lips around the head of my cock. Thrilled that I was erect again, I fingered her pussy for a moment, and then slid my finger deep into her ass. She responded by taking my entire shaft down her throat. I flicked my tongue against her clit.

She repeatedly forced my cock against the back of her throat.

No contrast.

I wouldn't want it any other way.

CHAPTER THIRTY-FOUR

LIV

Bound to his bed and blindfolded, I tightened my jaw as the leather straps of the flogger came down against the tender flesh of my ass. I knew better than to make a sound.

I was so turned on that my nipples coming in contact with the comforter was enough to drive me insane. He gripped my hair tight in his hand, twisted my head to the side and pressed his muscular chest into my back.

"I'm going to fuck that tight little pussy of yours," he whispered into my ear.

Please do.

Please.

"Anything to please you, Sir."

The faint sound of something whistling through the air caused my muscles to tense. Another swat on my ass – this time the unmistakable feeling of the crop.

My pussy throbbed so hard it ached.

I needed Luke inside of me. I needed to feel his thick cock filling me, stretching me, making me whole.

Again, the crop against the other side of my ass.

Silence.

He forced a finger inside of me. I opened my mouth and breathed silently into the comforter, pleased to have him grace me with penetration. He added another finger, pushed deep into my aching twat, and then slowly pulled them free.

"Open," he said.

I stretched my mouth wide.

The sweet taste of my pussy against my tongue drove me into a frenzy. I readily sucked his fingers free of my wetness, hoping he would once again give me the satisfaction of having them deep within me.

"Do you want that cock?" he asked.

"Yes," I begged.

His weight lifted from my back. A faint rustle from beside me caused me to tilt my head to the side in wonder.

The shrill whistle of the crop provided warning, but not soon enough. My muscles tensed from the sharp but erotic pain that filled me. I chewed against my lip and prepared for another swat.

His chest pressed into my back. His hand tugged against my hair. "Do you want that cock?" he whispered into my ear.

"Yes, Sir," I barked.

"That's better," he breathed.

Having my eyesight deprived didn't necessarily make the sex better, only different. I definitely wouldn't want to be blind on a permanent basis, but being blindfolded on occasion was proving to be an exciting addition to our BDSM play.

Slowly, we were both becoming comfortable with our sexual selves. Together, we read, watched videos, and experimented. We always agreed on what we were going to do, and made clear what we wouldn't allow. My safe word, *almond butter*, had yet to pass my lips.

I felt his weight lift from against my back, only to be replaced by the feeling of his thighs against the backs of my legs.

Please.

Please fuck me

I wasn't in a mental place where I felt I wanted his dick, or that I preferred him to fuck me over some other act.

I needed it.

My twat ached.

Fill me with that big fat cock.

The pressure of the head of his dick against my wet pussy lips didn't last long. With ease, he slid his length inside of me. With my legs bound to opposite corners at the foot of the bed, and my hands bound to the head, I was his for the taking.

And take me he certainly did.

He drove himself in and out of my willing pussy in a steady rhythmic pace. Long steady strokes of his thick cock filled me completely, satisfying me to no end. I clenched my eyes closed and focused on the feeling of his balls banging against my clit with each stroke.

Although we had tried orgasm control on many occasions, tonight I was free to have an orgasm whenever I wanted.

But I wasn't free to speak unless spoken to.

I loved dirty talk, and over time, we had both become quite good at turning each other on with our sexual banter.

"You may speak freely," he said as he continued to fuck me steadily.

I arched my back, lifted my head from the bed, and wet my lips.

"Fuck me, Sir. Fuck me hard."

"Use my pussy like only you know how."

His rhythm increased. His breathing became labored slightly.

"Take what is yours," I wailed.

His thick cock stretched me open, sending a pleasurable ache through me.

"I love that big cock, Sir," I cried. "I do."

"I'm going to fill you with cum," he bellowed.

"Please do, Sir," I begged.

He pounded himself into me savagely, causing the restraints on my feet to pull against my ankles. Every muscle in my legs and ass shook with each vicious stroke.

At his current pace, I knew I wouldn't last long, and I didn't.

As I felt myself begin to clench against his cock, I craned my neck, pointing my mouth toward the ceiling.

"Fill my tight little pussy, Sir. I beg you," I pleaded.

As my body convulsed into an orgasm from deep within my soul, his cock swelled. One more stroke, and he held still, his cum bursting from the tip and filling me as I reached a new level of climax.

Exhausted, he collapsed onto me. A tingling ran through me from my nipples to my clit.

I blinked my eyes repeatedly as he removed the blindfold. Although the room was dim, my eyes adjusted slowly to the light. As I watched him unfasten the restraints, I grinned.

"I love it when you fuck me."

"And I love fucking you," he said. "Give me just a minute, and we'll take a bath."

"I can't wait."

He lifted me from the bed, carried me to the bathroom, and rubbed my back as we waited for the tub to fill.

Luke was my lover, my therapist, and my Sir.

But, above all, he was still my best friend.
And I loved him dearly for it.

CHAPTER THIRTY-FIVE

LUKE

The home I made every effort to stay away from hadn't changed one bit, but I had. Confronting my mother seemed to free me of whatever had haunted me for a lifetime. I hadn't walked along the beach at midnight seeking refuge from my dreams for over three months.

"Pass the salad, Liv," Matt said.

"Only if you'll pass the cottage cheese," she said. "I'll trade."

My mind drifted to the recollection of the cottage cheese on the night Liv told me she was done dating. I smiled to myself at the thought of that night being the predecessor to our relationship.

"Cottage cheese is ugly," I said jokingly as she passed it to Matt.

"I know," she said. "But it tastes so good."

Not only had I returned to my childhood home, it seemed I was doing so eagerly. Matt, Liv, and I had a standing Sunday dinner with my father, which was something I never would have guessed. Matt was walking with a cane, my father was surfing every day, and Liv was working part-time out of my shop – designing graphics for surfboards across the nation.

It took some time for it to happen, but as far as I was concerned, my life was perfect.

I raised my fork and wagged it at my father. "The chicken is spot-on,

Dad."

He looked up from his plate and tossed his hair out of his eyes. "Well, I've had a while to perfect it."

"It's scrumptious," Liv said.

"I'm glad you like it. Better than that pork we had last week." He chuckled. "Bunch of sore asses that night."

"Try getting up and down off that toilet with a cane," Matt complained.

My father had prepared pork tacos the previous week, and everyone got terribly ill immediately after the meal. The bathrooms occupied all night until Liv and I felt safe enough to try and venture home.

My father took a drink of water and peered over the table. "So I hit Black's twice this week. West north-west swell kicked in and I caught six footers all day Wednesday. Thursday wasn't as good, but better than Scripps."

"Better stay away from Black's, Old Man. You're liable to get hurt," I said.

He cocked an eyebrow. "Who taught your skinny little ass to surf?"

I shrugged. "A long time ago."

"Just like riding a bike," he said. "And I didn't teach you everything I know."

"Sounds like a challenge," Liv said.

"Sure does," Matt chimed.

I pointed to the plate in front of my father. "Toss me a piece of chicken."

My father picked up a chicken breast and tossed it high into the air. As I watched it reach its apex and begin to fall, Liv poked me in the ribs.

I flinched, and the chicken fell directly into my lap.

"Looks like you're the one getting old. You've got slow hands," my father said.

I reached into my lap and picked up the chicken. "She poked me."

"Sounds like an excuse," he said. "And you know what I say about excuses."

"What's that?" Liv asked.

"They're like assholes," he said. "Everybody has one, and they all stink."

"I did poke him," Liv said.

My dad shrugged. "He's losing his touch."

After dusting the lint from the piece of chicken, without warning, I tossed it across the table at my father. With lightning quick speed, he raised his hand and snatched the chicken out of the air.

"Impressive for an old man," I said.

He threw the chicken at me.

It hit me dead center in the chest.

I threw it back.

He caught it, grinned, and took a bite.

"Alright, you two," Liv said.

My relationship with my father was always a good one, but my mother's actions caused me to spend more time away from the home than I really wanted to. After she left, I continued to stay away, as the home reminded me of her and of the abuse.

As a result, my father, who had done nothing but support me for my entire life, suffered. Having him in my life again made me feel young. It seemed I was now living my childhood with him that I felt I had been deprived of.

"So one of these days you two are going to have to get married,

FUCK BUDDY

Liv," my dad said.

She looked up from her plate. "Why's that?"

He poked a slice of cucumber with his fork and lifted it halfway to his mouth. "I want a grandkid. Kids keep us young."

"We don't have to get married to make babies," she said.

He dropped his fork. After it clanked onto the edge of his plate, he turned to face me and scowled.

"Don't tell me you two are having sex out of wedlock," he said stone-faced.

I shook my head. "Not a chance."

I glanced at Liv.

She swallowed heavily.

My dad shifted his gaze to her. "So, you were joking, right?"

She glanced at me with wide eyes, obviously looking for some type of support.

I shrugged.

"I uhhm." She turned to face my dad. "Can I plead the fifth?"

He shrugged and gazed down at his plate. "Just as well admit guilt."

"Luke?" she whined.

"Can't help ya, Babe."

My father glanced at Matt, shifted his eyes to me, and then to Liv. With his eyes glued on Liv, he continued to torture her. "Well. Personally, I wouldn't fuck him with Hillary Clinton's twat. Did he tell you about the herpes?"

"Herpes?" she snapped back.

She turned to me and scowled.

I shook my head.

"How long's it been since you had an outbreak, Son?"

"Leave her alone," I said.

"Or what?" he laughed. "You gonna toss another piece of chicken at me?"

Liv turned toward me and cleared her throat. "So it was a joke, right?"

"Yeah," I said. "Did you forget how ornery he is?"

"I guess so," she said.

Everyone had a laugh, and we continued to pick at our food until we were full. As we sat and exchanged glances, everyone too stuffed to move, Liv pushed her chair from the table slightly and peered toward my father.

"So," Liv said. "Did Luke tell you he sold the shop?"

He coughed. "Come again?"

"The shop. He sold it. Got, what Luke?" She turned toward me. "Two hundred and fifty thousand?"

"Two hundred and fifty thousand?" he howled. "For beach front property?"

He glared at me.

I shrugged. "I thought it was a good deal. Some guy had been pestering me about it, and Liv and I talked about it. We were going to tell you the other day, but we all ended up shittin' our pants after that pork, and hell, I forgot."

He glared at Liv.

"So," she said. "We're moving to South Dakota."

"South Dakota? What in the absolute fuck is in South fucking Dakota?" he fumed.

"Snowmen. We can build snowmen."

"Who wants to build fucking snowmen?" he snapped back.

FUCK BUDDY

He alternated glances between Liv and me. Matt continued to pick at his salad, paying little attention to any of what was said.

"Luke and me," she said. "It'll make for great Christmas mornings with the kids."

"What kids?" he asked.

She shrugged. "Your grandkids."

He wrinkled his nose. "Are you fucking with me?"

"About South Dakota or the kids?" she asked.

He pressed his forearms against the edge of the table and leaned forward, keeping his eyes locked on her the entire time.

"Both," he responded.

"Yes," she said.

He glared at her for a moment, realized it was all a joke, and reached for the last remaining piece of chicken. Sans any announcement or warning, he tossed it directly at her chest.

She caught the chicken in mid-flight.

"Thanks," she said.

And she took a bite.

I guess the martial arts lessons are paying off after all.

Together, Liv and I shared a love for the ocean, each other, family, and great sex. We may have lacked contrast, but I wouldn't have had it any other way. Being in love with a woman who shared my interests, loves, and desires was priceless.

The only thing possible that could have made it any better would be to have her as my wife.

I snapped my fingers. "Dad?"

His eyes widened.

"It's time," I said.

He stood, walked around the edge of the table, and reached into his pocket. One of the many disadvantages of wearing board shorts, I had learned over the years, was the lack of pockets.

Liv wrinkled her nose and exchanged glances between us. "What are you two doing?"

I grinned. "It's time."

"Time for what?" she asked.

"Time for us to start having sex the legal way." I chuckled.

"What does that mean?" she asked.

I lowered myself to one knee, reached for her hand, and licked my increasingly dry lips.

"Liv." I gazed into her green eyes. "We're lovers, best friends, and undoubtedly soul mates. But one thing we're not, is married."

She gazed down at me as she chewed against her bottom lip.

"Liv, will you marry me?"

"I will," she blubbered.

I slipped the ring on her finger.

"Still have a spare bedroom." My father laughed. "You're welcome to use it."

"Oh, we'll use it," Liv said as she shifted her eyes from the ring to my father. "You can bet on that. Do you have any restraints or a whip you're not using?"

"I hope that's a joke," he said dryly.

A year prior, I never would have considered sleeping in my old room. But I had reached a point in my life where I truly felt I had recovered from my past.

As I picked her up from her seat and carried her down the hallway, I knew very little for certain.

FUCK BUDDY

But I knew one thing for sure.

We'd remain best friends until we died.

And all I could do was hope that when that day came, we were in each other's arms.

EPILOGUE

I gazed toward the horizon and shaded my eyes.

"Your dad is an awesome surfer," I said.

Matt turned toward me and grinned. "Always has been. Hell, he taught Luke."

Inside the tube with his arms outstretched, the water barreled immediately behind him, almost catching his right shoulder as it cascaded down at his side.

He rode the wave, high on the shoulder, until it diminished to nothing.

A few moments later, as he paddled out to catch another, Luke got up on a nice wave. The off shore winds had been picking up, and with them came the good waves.

As Luke steadied himself on the board, he held his arm outstretched, dragging it along the edge of the wave as if taunting it to attempt to break him. I grinned, knowing Luke was too in tune with himself to allow any wave to bring him down.

He carved back and forth, finding his perfect spot halfway up the face. As the wave reached its crest, the crowd began to stand and cheer.

Come on, Baby. You can do it.

It was undoubtedly the best wave of the day, and I wasn't the only one who was seeing it.

"Come on, Luke!" Juan shouted.

He swatted at the lower part of the tube as the board carved to the right, slapping some of the whitewater to his side.

The crowd, many of which stared through binoculars, went wild. On their feet cheering and shouting, most had come to see Luke, if even for one day.

He hadn't gone pro, but had agreed to surf for a day with his father as a show, giving one hundred percent of whatever anyone wanted to donate to a foundation for abused children. Over a thousand people showed up, and News 8 was there, in hopes of him agreeing to go pro.

Matt, Juan, and me knew he never would, but it was funny to listen to the people beg him to.

A few moments after the wave washed ashore, a man approached us.

"Mrs. Luke Eagan?" he asked.

I shielded my eyes and glanced up. "Yes?"

"Mike Trell with Riptide. Any chance you could talk your husband into an interview after the show?"

I shook my head. "I doubt it."

"Are you sure?" he asked.

I shrugged. "Sorry."

"Has the date been set for the next show? Rumor has it he'll be doing another," he asked.

Luke agreed to do another, but I really didn't want to be bothered. I was hot, I was tired, and my back hurt.

"I have no idea." I said, turning to face the horizon.

As he walked away, Matt turned to face me.

"When's the big day?" he asked.

"For the next show? Or," I paused and patted my hand against my stomach.

"I know when the show is," he said. "For the baby."

"Oh," I said as I rubbed my hand against my stomach. "November 2nd."

"Know the sex?" he asked.

I nodded my head. "I do. But sorry, we're not telling."

"Figures," he said as he turned to face the beach.

As Luke carried his board up the beach, I stood and grinned; proud of him for what he had done for charity. In no time our son would be learning to surf, spending his days and nights at the beach just like his father.

Luke stuck his board in the sand and ran toward us, waving off autographs and interviews along the way. There was no doubt in my mind that our baby would grow up to be just as stubborn, just as proud, and just as humble as Luke.

And I wouldn't want him any other way.

Printed in Great Britain
by Amazon